FATAL FESTIVE DONUTS

A DONUT TRUCK COZY MYSTERY

CINDY BELL

ISBN-13: 978-1981174430

ISBN-10: 1981174435

CONTENTS

inter was in full swing throughout the town of Marsail, and Brenda was quite happy about it, even though her cheeks were red, and her toes were cold buried deep inside her thick winter boots and underneath two pairs of socks. Sometimes she got a little tired of the cold weather, but most of the time she enjoyed it. Especially, if it snowed. However so far, there had been nothing but chilly days without a flake in the sky, and it was almost Christmas. The chance of a good strong storm faded with every day that passed. As another icy wind carried through the parking lot, a shiver coursed through her. She tightened the fluffy scarf around her neck and tried to get it tucked down into the collar of her jacket. No matter how hard she tried, the cool breeze still managed to get right down her shirt. She shivered and wrapped her arms around herself as she hurried towards the truck.

"You're not cold, are you?" Joyce peered over at her with a half-smile. "It's practically spring weather out today."

"Spring weather?" Brenda gazed at her, her mouth half-open. "It's freezing out here!"

"Freezing is a bit of an exaggeration." Joyce offered a mirthful smirk. "A nip in the air is the best way to start the day, that's what I always say."

"Tucked in my warm bed is the best place for me today. I usually enjoy the winter weather, but this is just a bit too chilly." She shivered again as she walked closer to the truck. The sight of it pleased her so much, that she almost forgot about how cold it was. The cheerful donuts painted along the side of their new truck seemed to sparkle with all of the Christmas lights bouncing off it. There it was, her very own business. Well, her business that she shared with Joyce. It made her so proud to see it on display among the other trucks that lined the long street. The holiday market was in full swing, and they'd managed to score a coveted space in the line of food vendors. Brenda was filled with excitement. They were off to a good start, but she was curious about exactly how well they would do during the market.

It was impossible to deny the joy that spread throughout the cheerfully decorated section of town. Even the most reserved person could be swayed by giant candy canes, a good amount of garland, and the seasonal music that played through the speakers that had been erected. Later in the day there would be a Santa Claus set up for the children to visit. She felt a pang as she missed the opportunity to see Sophie sit on Santa's lap this year. That was one of the drawbacks about going back to work. She had to miss a few special moments here and there. But not once had she regretted it. She felt enlivened by having so many new responsibilities, and fascinated by the possibilities of what the future might hold. Sophie had her own new experiences as she started her first year in school, and that was exciting in itself.

"Look, they put new lights up along the walkway." Brenda smiled. "They haven't turned them on yet, but when they do they will be amazing. I'm so glad we decided to go ahead with the ornament donuts, I think they are going to be a huge hit."

"It was your brilliant idea to team up with a local artist to sell tiny ornaments along with the decorated gingerbread donuts. I never would have thought of that." Joyce cast a smile in her direction.

"I just figured if people are here to shop, then they might be swayed into buying a treat that comes with a decoration as well. And who can turn down a hand-painted ornament?"

"I'm not one for ornaments, to be honest. I get one of those prelit trees. It's great. I just pop it out of the box, then put it up, and Christmas is done."

"There's certainly nothing wrong with that. I think once Sophie is grown up, I'll be more likely to want an easy tree. But right now, everything about Christmas just seems so magical, and I want to enjoy that with her while it lasts." She smiled at the thought of her daughter's shocked eyes on Christmas morning. "All of the presents, and her favorite part is still finding the cookies with bites taken out of them."

"Oh boy, that must be a wonderful moment to share with her." Joyce winked. "Kids, they really don't stay young long, so you're absolutely right to savor the time you have with them."

"I wonder what it will be like when she has children of her own." Her mind wandered for a moment as they approached the truck. The entire street had been closed off for the holiday market.

"That is something to be curious about. I imagine if she's a mother like you, her kids will be just as wonderful. Have you and Charlie thought about having another?" Joyce cast a curious glance in her direction.

"Oh, no. Not really." She cleared her throat. "It's hard to even think about it when we are both busy, and Sophie is such a great kid, it seems I don't know, wrong, to shake things up?"

"You think that. But life has a way of changing our minds about things." Joyce shrugged. "I suppose time will tell."

"Yes, I think you're right about that. Oh look, there are more trees up at the tree stand! Great timing, I wanted to buy a tree today. I've been looking forward to picking one out. I'm glad they decided to have a tree stand here, but I wonder who's running it?" Brenda peered at the fenced in area, but didn't notice anyone near the cash register at the front.

"Remember, it's Gray Spruel, they introduced him at the vendors meeting. It surprises me because one of the locals said that since he's moved here they didn't think he's left his farm much. But he does sell trees off it during the season. At least, I've heard he does. I've never been on his property myself." Joyce looked in the direction of the tree stand. "I'm not so sure it'll be great having him here. He has a reputation for being standoffish. I personally do my best to avoid him as he simply has a gruff look about him."

"That surprises me, Joyce, you always strike me as so open. You'd really judge him by how he looks?" She raised her eyebrows in genuine shock.

"Normally, I do my best not to judge, but once you see this man you'll understand. There's just something about him that makes me very uneasy. I don't know how to explain it." She wiped her hands together and shuddered. "It's like I'm covered in spiderwebs."

"Hmm, do you get that feeling with anyone else?" She studied her friend.

"A few other people, yes. Not often though. That's why when I felt it around him, I paid attention to it. I know it may seem wrong to you, but sometimes you have to trust your gut. And from the stories I've heard about him over the last couple of weeks, I don't think my instincts are far off." She frowned. "You'll have to decide what you think for yourself, though."

"I guess I will." Brenda looked back at the tree stand, then glanced at her watch. "It's early, but I think he might already be open. We have a little time before we need to get things started for opening. I'm going to go take a look at the trees for a few minutes if you don't mind. We still need one for the house. I wasn't sure if we should get one, since Sophie is already with my parents, but seeing as we are having Christmas lunch at my house and the fact that I like to leave it up for as long as I can after Christmas, I think I should. It's nice having it there for New Year's."

"That's true. I don't usually take mine down until mid-January, but that could be procrastination not celebration." She laughed. "Go on and take a look. I'll get things started on the truck."

"Thanks!" Brenda walked off towards the trees. A warm feeling still brewed within her from the time she spent with Joyce. Since Brenda's bathrooms were being retiled and Joyce lived closer to the holiday market, which was on the outskirts of town, they decided that Brenda should camp out at Joyce's place. With her daughter away with her parents, and Charlie so busy, it was the easiest way. She'd been a little nervous at first, because she wasn't sure if she and Joyce would get along well if they were together all the time, but so far it had been better than she ever could have expected. Even though Joyce was a lot older than her, in many ways she felt as if she was like the sister she never had.

As Joyce continued towards the truck she smiled to herself. She loved that she had the chance to be part of Brenda's family, even if it was mostly through hearing stories and sharing memories. It brought a part of her alive that she had tucked away long ago.

~

When Brenda walked up to the register, she looked around for Gray. She didn't see any sign of him.

"Hello?" She peered around some of the trees. Just then she heard a loud bang, loud enough to make her jump. As the sensation bolted through her body, her breath caught in her throat. She spun around and came face to face with a man as large, wide, and hairy as a grizzly bear.

"Oh my!" She stumbled back, and slammed into a tree, which began to tip over.

He thrust his arm forward, his rough, thick fingers headed straight for her face. She was too frightened to even manage to scream. His hand continued past her and caught the tree before it could topple the rest of the way behind her.

"Careful there. You bruise it, you buy it." His dark brown eyes squinted at her from beneath bushy eyebrows.

"Sorry." She caught her breath and moved a few steps away from him. "Something startled me."

"Yeah, I was opening up the stand. I didn't know there was anyone here already." He brushed his hand off on the thick, plaid jacket he wore.

"I wasn't sure if you would be here so early."

"I come in about five-thirty every morning. I set up all of the trees and water them."

"Oh, I hadn't noticed you."

"I try to keep to myself. Some of the vendors are upset with me because I got such a large area at the market. I don't like to get involved in that stuff. Anyway, are you looking for a tree?"

"Yes, I think so."

"You think so?" He chuckled, but it was a bit rough. "Let me know if you decide you want one. I've got other things to do."

He turned and walked back off to his truck. She was a little unnerved. Joyce had been right, the man did send off a very unsettling vibe. Whether it was his size, or his demeanor, he didn't exactly strike her as friendly. She shook it off, and focused on finding a tree. Whether or not he had good customer service skills, he had some beautiful trees to choose from.

The branches of the pine trees greeted her with soft brushes against her jacket as she walked through the make-shift tree farm. No, it wasn't the same thing as trekking up some mountain with an ax to cut down her very own tree, but personally, she preferred the convenience and safety of picking one out in a parking lot. There were so many to choose from that she wished her husband, Charlie was there to give her his opinion. He'd encouraged her to pick one out on her own as he was caught up in a story and couldn't spare even a few minutes. She was used to this chaos around the holidays. They were the prime time for heartfelt and hard-hitting articles, both of which he dreaded, but was always asked to dig up. Even though he tended to report mostly on economic and political issues, the newspaper tapped all of their journalists for content as Christmas approached. She'd become accus-tomed to the late hours and sometimes multi-day absences. This was the first year since Sophie had been born that she was working, too.

As Brenda reached out to touch the needles on one of the trees she recalled Sophie's first Christmas.

She'd wanted it to be perfect, but it turned into a mess. She'd spent hours decorating the tree, only to have Charlie accidently knock it over when he was hanging more lights on it on Christmas Eve. Many of her ornaments shattered, and she felt as if her baby's first Christmas had been ruined. But Sophie didn't even seem to notice. All she wanted was wrapping paper to crinkle and something to put in her mouth. It was the first of many humbling parenting lessons that she would face. The thought of being away from her during the holidays had given her some pause, but she knew that her parents would be more than happy to whisk her around to all of the holiday events in their town, and she would be busy with the market.

A sharp voice drew her attention.

"I don't want to hear another word about it."

The words carried through the branches of the full tree she had her eye on. A moment later she recognized it as belonging to a man she knew, Jerry. Her skin crawled with annoyance the moment she recognized it. Jerry owned the bakery in the area. He had voiced his strong dislike at the fact that they had allowed the donut truck at the market. He had applied for a spot and it had been given to 'Donuts on the Move' instead. The market organizers had said that it was because

11

donuts were in high demand and that people could still go to the bakery. They especially liked the fact that the truck made both fried and baked donuts. Jerry had believed that it was stealing his business and the spot should be his. She recalled the argument they'd gotten into a few days before. He made it very clear that he felt that she and Joyce shouldn't have been allowed the spot, he was a local after all.

While Joyce understood his concern to an extent, the fact was that if they hadn't got the business then it would have been given to another bakery, donut or pastry stand. Besides, even though they both made donuts, the bakery sold many more products, so she didn't know why he was so concerned. Business was business, she needed the business.

Jerry stood on the sidewalk in front of his bakery and shouted at them both as they tried to serve customers. Joyce was so fed up she was ready to call the police for harassment, but Brenda had talked her out of it. She didn't want to have a big feud brew between them and was certain that she could have a rational conversation with him that would lead to a peaceful conclusion. She couldn't have been more wrong. He barely let her say a word and barked at her as if she were a child. At some point his words blended together into just noise as she realized that there was no reasoning with him. When she returned to the truck, defeated, Joyce had again offered to call the police, but Brenda insisted they play it by ear. Maybe he would calm down. Maybe he would accept that they weren't going to move the truck.

Hearing his voice as she looked over the tree, made all of that tension course through her muscles, yet again.

A second voice, responded, just as sharply.

"I won't be dismissed like this. Do you understand me? I practically built that bakery from the ground up. You would have never succeeded without me. You can't just push me out like this."

She recognized the voice as belonging to Orville, a man she was more familiar with, as he was most often at the bakery. Since she had started working at the market she had stopped in a few times just to pick something up and he'd been quite cordial to her, the complete opposite of Jerry. He didn't sound cordial now, however. She knew she shouldn't be eavesdropping, but she was curious about why they were fighting, and with Jerry's temper she wondered what he might do if things grew any more tense.

"I can do whatever I please. I'm the owner of the bakery, and that's part of the problem, you never could get that through your thick skull. You don't get to tell me what to do. I'm the owner, not you. If you had a problem with my decisions you should have kept your mouth shut. Instead you disrespected me in front of my employees, and questioned my authority, as if you had any right to do that." His voice raised an octave or two.

"Your decision was reckless, and put the business at risk. Yes, you're the owner, but you're not the only one that relies on this business. If you do something to harm it, then we're all at risk of losing our jobs. All I did was point out that you were making a mistake by deciding to put that stall out there and..."

"Enough! I don't want to hear anything else from you. You've been fired, and as far as I'm concerned now you are harassing me. If you contact me in any way again, I will call the police to handle the situation."

As he stormed away from Orville, she could see that his muscles were tense. Orville stared after him, his eyes low, and his shoulders slumped. She felt a good deal of empathy for him as she knew he was passionate about his job. Whatever happened between Jerry and Orville, she couldn't believe that it was so bad that Orville deserved to be fired. However, it also wasn't her business. As she turned her attention back to the trees she tried not to think about Jerry's temper or the consequences that Orville faced. Instead she felt the needles of a nearby tree and considered what height would work best in the living room. Once she'd finally selected a tree, she headed to the register. She wasn't so sure if she was ready to face Gray again, but her policy was always to kill people with kindness.

"Hi!" She called out and waved the ticket she'd pulled off the tree. "Gray?"

He lumbered up from behind his truck.

"How do you know my name?" He eyed her.

"Oh, I must have heard it." She shrugged.

"Do you want a tree?"

"I'd like to buy this tree, but I won't be able to pick it up until later in the week. Is that all right?"

"It's your tree once you pay for it, maybe I should charge you storage?" He quirked a brow, then his lips spread wide enough to reveal his teeth. It took her a second to realize he was smiling.

"I hope not." She laughed.

"Just write your name on the card, and I'll make sure I set it aside for you. If you want, I can deliver it."

"Let me guess, that's an extra charge?" She grinned.

"Yeah, that's right. Ten bucks." He nodded.

"Oh okay, yes, let's add that on." She wrote her name down on the card and handed it to him. "Thanks a lot."

"Thank you, Brenda." He looked at the card for a moment.

She smiled again, then handed over the money for the tree. Maybe he wasn't going to win any customer service awards, but she saw potential.

CHAPTER 2

*A*s Joyce walked closer to the truck, she noticed a small stall had been erected a few feet away from it. The wooden structure was tiny enough to be portable, but brightly painted, and featured images of all kinds of pastries. The sight startled her. There were various stalls throughout the market, but they were spaced apart according to regulation and the comfort of customers. The stall was positioned practically in the same space that the truck occupied. It only took her a moment longer to realize that the stall was hosted by the nearby bakery.

"Jerry," Joyce growled his name. She assumed this was his way of fighting back against the truck getting the spot at the market and being parked, in his opinion, too close to his bakery. Brenda had tried to reason with him, but Joyce had warned her that he was simply an unreasonable man. Now, she would handle it. As she marched towards the stall she already had quite a few things that she planned to say. However, as she approached the stall she was disappointed to discover two young men, instead of Jerry, who was at least in his fifties. She recognized them as employees from his bakery. As she walked towards them she tried to lip read some of their conversation. She grew up with three older brothers, who often plotted against her. In order to protect herself against their pranks, she had learnt to lip read and prank them first. She had honed the skill over the years. As she walked towards the stall she could lip read a few snippets, but at the angle they were standing away from her she couldn't discern a lot. She could tell that they were angry and that they were talking about Orville. She walked closer to the stall so she could try to hear their conversation.

"All I'm saying is that it's wrong that he fired him. Orville has worked for the bakery the longest, he got me my job there, why would he just fire him like that?" The older of the two, she recalled his name was Mark, seemed quite upset.

"I get it, Mark, but there's nothing that you can

do about it. Jerry does whatever he wants. Orville was arguing with him, he knows better than that." He frowned. "It's best to stay out of it, or you're going to be the next one to go."

"For what? Having an opinion?" Mark rolled his eyes. "Clarence, if he can just up and fire Orville like that, nothing I can do is going to keep my job safe. But am I just supposed to keep my mouth shut when he does something like that? You and I both know that Orville is the one who runs the bakery, he does all of the hard work and the advertising. It just isn't right."

"I know, I know it isn't right." Clarence held his hands out in surrender. "But there's nothing that we can do. You just have to accept that. I want to keep my job. Don't you want to keep yours?"

"Yes, you know I do." He sighed. "But still, I feel like there should be something we could do. What is wrong with Jerry, anyway? Did he just have a really bad life or something?"

"If you're looking for a psychological explanation, I have no clue. Man, some people are just not great people. I don't know anything about him, other than he's my boss. I'm not sure that I want to know anything more."

Joyce's blood boiled as she heard their words.

She hated to think of anyone being mistreated. She was tempted to join in on the conversation. She had plenty to say about Jerry's awful customer service skills, and his impossible behavior. She could suggest that they document the hostility in their workplace, and perhaps report him to the authorities. But she knew it would be unprofessional to discuss such things with Jerry's employees. In her experience, young men didn't always want to hear her opinion on things anyway. She turned on her heel and walked back towards the truck.

'Donuts on the Move' had been a lifesaver for her. Just when she thought she would lose herself to the grief of her husband's death, she came up with the idea to invest some of the money from his life insurance in a business. She'd always wanted to take a chance on something, and when she decided it would be a food truck, she knew exactly who she wanted as the baker. She'd tasted Brenda's cakes and pastries quite a few times as she always made items for the bake sales, or to donate to charitable events, and sometimes just to cheer up someone who was having a hard time. She had a talent for baking, though she wasn't fully aware of how good she was at it. She managed to create everything with love, and that love could be tasted in every fluffy, sweet bite of the goodies she created. Since agreeing to work together, they'd become close friends despite the fact that Brenda was much younger than her, and perhaps it was her friendship with Brenda, more than the donut truck itself, that brought back her enjoyment of life.

However, Jerry was threatening that enjoyment. She tried to put thoughts of him out of her mind as she reached the truck. She knew that no matter what he did he couldn't recreate the same delicious taste that Brenda did, so there was nothing to be concerned about.

"Joyce!" She glanced over to see Brenda approaching from the tree stand. Her cheeks were flushed as her gaze fixated on the new stall not far from the truck.

"I know!" Joyce rolled her eyes. "Jerry strikes again!"

"I can't believe he did this. He knows this isn't allowed. He has to be approved to get the spot. This is totally against regulations." Brenda crossed her arms.

"I'm sure that he does know that. But maybe he is just trying his luck. Maybe he doesn't care." She sighed. "I am not one to go down quietly."

"Joyce, maybe we should just let things play out.

The organizers will see the stall soon enough and I really don't think that their stall being there is going to hurt our sales one bit. People have already tasted our food, and they like it, so why make a big fight out of it?" She winced. "I'm afraid if we make enemies we're going to have a lot of trouble continuing on here. Jerry is a pain, if we make too much of a scene he might just come back at us harder."

"You make a good point." Joyce nodded. "But he might not be willing to play it nice. He may just continue to harass us, and at some point, that will have to be stopped."

"Let's just do our best to have a good day, and not think about him. If he tries to make any trouble, we'll make sure that the police arrive to stop it. Deal?" Brenda thrust her hand out to her.

"Deal." She took it in a firm shake, then grimaced. "Ugh, what is that? You're all sticky!"

"Oops." Brenda blushed. "I must have gotten some sap on me from the trees. I'm so sorry. Let's go get cleaned up." She started to climb up on the step that led to the door of the truck.

"Wait!" Joyce grabbed her by the elbow. "Watch out!"

"What?" She jumped back, eyes wide.

"The eggs, they've already been delivered."

Joyce picked up a crate of eggs that was left on the step.

"Wow, that's a big change." Brenda grinned. "Usually they don't get here until closer to noon. Great job, Aaron!"

"I know, I think I like this new delivery man. He manages to get everything here on time, or even early. Now we won't have to worry about running out of eggs."

As Brenda unlocked the door, she laughed as she glanced back at her. "No, but we might have to worry about them freezing out here." She swung the door open and stepped aside to allow Joyce inside. "See, our day is already improving. Well, aside from the sticky hands." She glanced at her hands and shrugged.

"All right, all right, I'm letting it go, I'm being positive." Joyce winked at Brenda.

"You always manage to be positive."

"Sometimes I think you're a bad influence on me with your sunshiny personality."

"Hmm, I can't help it, you bring it out in me."

They both laughed as they took turns scrubbing their hands in the sink. It wasn't long before the first customers arrived, and as Brenda predicted, the stall beside their truck had no impact on their sales.

As Joyce and Brenda were about to close up shop for the evening, two figures walked towards the truck. From a distance it was difficult to make out who they were, since the lights strung along the walkway hadn't been turned on for the night, yet. However, when they got close to the window, Brenda recognized them right away.

"Clarence, Mark, how are you doing, tonight?" She greeted them with a bright smile. She didn't want them to think that there was any animosity between them even though they had been running the stall beside their truck.

"Pretty good." Mark smiled. "Can we buy some of those delicious gingerbread donuts, please? Six, if possible? Three with sprinkles, three with just glaze? Or are you all out?"

"Please say you're not." Clarence groaned and rubbed his stomach. "I can't live without at least a bite."

"Oh wow, I'm so glad you like them." Brenda laughed.

"Sorry boys, we're already closing down the register." Joyce thumbed through the cash before sliding it into a deposit envelope.

"That's all right, these will be on the house." Brenda packed them six donuts in a small colorful box. "Enjoy them."

"Thanks, we will." Mark grabbed the box and licked his lips. "I can't wait!"

"Thanks again," Clarence said. "You're the best."

"You're welcome, have a good night. See you in the morning!" She waved to them as they walked away.

"You're so kind." Joyce smiled at her. "I probably would have turned them away."

"Aw. I believe you attract more flies with honey, than with vinegar." She shrugged.

"We're running a food truck, don't say flies." Joyce laughed, and Brenda joined in with her.

"Good point."

"I think it's a good thing you did. They seem like good young men. I just hope that they will rub off on Jerry. Who surprisingly, hasn't been around much today, has he?" Joyce finished closing out the register.

"No, he hasn't. He must have hid out in the bakery, afraid we'd confront him or report him for the stall. See, now we have the upper hand." Brenda finished wiping down the counters.

"So you say, I hope that proves to be true." She

stepped down out of the truck.

Brenda turned back to lock the door. She was always careful to do it, as leaving the truck parked overnight in an unfamiliar area made her a little nervous.

"Let's get out of this cold!" She rushed to the car, with Joyce right beside her.

$\sim$

On the ride back to Joyce's house they sang Christmas songs together. Brenda had never laughed so hard. As she pulled into the driveway, she smiled at the thin string of lights that Joyce hung up around her patio. No, it wasn't extravagant, but it was just like Joyce, festive and to the point. Joyce unlocked the front door, and was immediately greeted by a floppy eared rabbit.

"Molly! I missed you today, my little fur ball." She scooped her up and carried her into the living room.

"You have such a lovely home, every time I come here I notice a new and wonderful detail." Brenda played a fingertip along the engraving of a wooden table. "What made you select this piece?"

"Actually, I didn't select it." Joyce offered a fond

smile as she ran her hand along the top of the side table. "This one my husband chose. He loved it, because he thought the etching looked like waves on the ocean. He was fond of the water, though not fond of boats." She laughed as she shook her head. "Once, I thought I would surprise him with a trip on a ferry. I got him all the way to the harbor, and the moment he saw the boat, he turned green. Poor fellow didn't have the heart to tell me that he got seasick so easily. He was actually going to get on the boat, but before he could set foot, he felt too sick and that ended that." She closed her eyes for a moment as she savored the memory. As unpleasant for him as it had been, it was one of her favorite times with him, mainly because she learned something new about the man that she thought she knew everything about.

"That's such a sweet story." Brenda gazed at the table a moment longer, then looked up at Joyce. "Charlie hasn't picked out a single piece of furniture at our house. That was always my job, while I was home with Sophie. I didn't mind it, but sometimes I wonder if he feels comfortable being surrounded by my choices."

"I'm sure he does. Sometimes men just aren't interested in that type of thing. Knowing how considerate you are, I would assume you took his likes and dislikes into consideration. I bet he feels like he is surrounded by your love." She winked. "It might sound a little cheesy, but it really is a beautiful thing. Special little moments, thoughtful gestures, those are the things that stay with you no matter how your life changes."

"Good advice to remember." Brenda took a deep breath, then expelled it. "I'm still wrestling with the decision to be away from Sophie during the holidays."

"I know that must be hard on you. If I could run the truck myself I would. But you know I don't bake." She grinned as she recalled the disaster her attempts had led to.

"No please, don't even think about it. I love being here with you, and I love working on the truck. This has been such an amazing experience for me. I guess it's just that with any change there will always be a little letting go of the way things once were. It doesn't mean I'm not happy with the way things are. I couldn't be more grateful."

"I feel the same way. I'm still amazed that things have worked out so well. Now, if we could just get rid of Jerry, we'd be doing even better." She rolled her eyes. "He's such a pain."

"Yes, he is one of the most difficult men I've ever run into, and I've dealt with a few over the years. I hate how he treats his employees. I don't know what makes him think that he can get away with things like that." Brenda frowned as she walked over to the couch and sat down.

"I don't know, but one of these days someone is going to teach him a lesson, and take him down a notch or two in the process."

"I just hope I'm around to see it." Brenda smiled.

"Normally, I have a rule about not wishing anything bad on anyone, but it's hard to follow it in Jerry's case. I keep trying to remind myself that he must have had some terrible things happen to him in his life to turn out so harsh, but that doesn't always work to keep my temper in check." Joyce frowned.

The furry rabbit hopped right up onto the couch beside her. As she squirmed into Brenda's lap, her ears flopped and wiggled, too.

"Oh, she is so, so cute. Sophie is dying to have one of her own." She stroked the rabbit's soft white fur. "But I'm not sure now is the right time."

"They are a bit of work, and you have to watch their nails, they can be quite sharp." Joyce reached out and pet the bunny as well. "But, she sure makes

29

me happy every time I see her, and that's worth it to me."

"I'm sure it is." Brenda smiled as she looked up at her and caught the glow in her blue eyes. In that moment she could picture Joyce as young as her six-year-old daughter, just as gleeful, and fascinated by a beautiful creature.

After Joyce and Brenda shared a light dinner, they both headed to bed early. In order to be at the truck on time the next morning they needed to be awake by four, and out the door by four-thirty. It was just a little earlier than they were used to, as normally they opened the truck at six. Since many people liked to arrive very early for the market, they decided to move the opening time up a bit to make sure they didn't miss any customers. As Brenda headed to bed that night, she shared a whispered conversation with her husband, who was still hard at work at the newspaper office. He often worked from home, but during these very busy times of year and due to their minor renovations, he had decided it was easier to be at the office.

Joyce snuggled Molly close to her, and whispered goodnight to the picture frame on the table beside her bed. It didn't matter that the picture was unable to respond, in her heart, he always would.

CHAPTER 3

The next morning, Brenda woke with a sense of determination. She was going to make friends with Jerry, even if it killed her. Whatever it took to get him on their side, she would figure out a way to make it happen. When she walked into the kitchen, she found Joyce already there with coffee made, and leftover scones from the day before. They feasted on them, and savored their coffee.

"You know getting up this early in the morning is kind of nice." Joyce smiled. "It's almost as if we get the world to ourselves, isn't it?"

"Yes, I agree. Most people are still asleep in their beds, and we're already up, enjoying the day. I could get used to this. I could also get used to skipping the rushing around getting everything ready for school craziness in the morning." She grinned.

"Oh, you would miss it, and you know it." Joyce rinsed their cups out in the sink, then set them in the dishwasher. "We'd better get moving if we're going to make it there early."

"Yes, I would miss it, you're right." She laughed as she gathered her things. "Let's have a great day, Joyce. No matter what."

They headed out the door to Brenda's car. She insisted that since she was staying at Joyce's she would be the one to do all the driving, so that Joyce wouldn't be out of gas money as well.

"Yes, I can agree to that. I just hope that Jerry doesn't cause any trouble. I'm in the mood to cause a little trouble right back." She pursed her lips as she settled in the car.

"Honey remember, Joyce." She started the engine and looked over at her. "Or at least, sugar. Is that better?"

"Fine, I'll do my best to smother him with sugar." She laughed.

When they arrived at the market there were a few other cars that dotted the parking lot, but most people hadn't arrived just yet. The two continued to joke and laugh as they approached the truck.

Brenda was absolutely glowing with joy. There was a time she would have shied away and done whatever Jerry barked at her to do. But that wasn't who she was anymore. She wasn't going to allow herself to be intimidated by anyone anymore, especially a man like him.

As she climbed up on the first step to unlock the door to the truck, she was filled with excitement for the day. Then she noticed something gooey all over the steps.

"Ugh, what is this?" She lifted her shoe to find the sole of it covered in something strange. Then she noticed the egg shells on the step, and all around the step on the ground. "Oh no, Aaron must have broken the eggs, or maybe something else got to them?" She sighed, but was determined not to let it affect their day. "It's all right, it's early enough to order some more."

"Still, he should be more careful." Joyce frowned.

"He might have been in a rush or something." As the key slid into the lock, Brenda discovered something shocking. "Joyce!" Her voice trembled.

"What is it?" She looked over at her with alarm. It wasn't often that Brenda sounded so frazzled.

"The door is unlocked." Brenda tugged it open

as she spoke. Perhaps she expected to see a robber beyond the door, or even some kind of crafty animal. Instead, she saw a body strewn across the floor of the truck. A body, that appeared to be Jerry.

Her head spun with fear and disbelief. Was it some kind of prank? Had someone just put a mannequin that looked like Jerry on the floor of their truck? It couldn't really be him, could it? She shuddered as she continued to stare.

"Is he dead?" The words spilled out of her mouth, though she couldn't believe she'd really spoken them.

"It sure looks like it." Joyce frowned as she finally overcame the shock of the sight of him. She reached down and checked for a pulse in his neck. Upon feeling nothing, she grabbed her phone and at the same time as she shouted for help from others who were just arriving, she dialed the emergency number for an ambulance. When she'd touched Jerry, his skin was cold. She was certain that it was too late for his life to be saved, but she knew that she had to at least try. As she gave the information to the person who answered her call, she noticed that Brenda had barely moved a muscle. She placed one hand on her back.

"It's going to be okay, Brenda, everything's going to be okay."

Brenda shivered at the touch and finally blinked. Her eyes burned from staring so hard at Jerry.

"How could this happen? A heart attack?" A quick glance over his body revealed no indication of any bodily harm. He was in his fifties, and as tightly wound as he was, she guessed it was possible that the stress in his life might have led to a heart attack.

"Maybe, or a stroke. It could be any number of things, but the important thing right now is that we get the authorities here."

"What's happened?" Mark ran towards the donut truck. He stopped short when he saw Jerry sprawled across the floor. "Is that Jerry?" His voice cracked.

"Yes, I'm afraid it is." Joyce was flustered as she attempted to answer him, while also trying to speak to the person on the phone. Mark knelt down and started doing CPR. Joyce knew it was pointless, but she knew he had to try. More people approached the scene. She knew that in a matter of seconds the news would spread and the crowd would be overwhelming.

"Please hurry." She hung up the phone and

tucked it into her pocket. In the distance she could already hear sirens.

"What was he doing here?" Brenda mumbled as she began to shift from one foot to the other. "How could he end up on our floor? I'm sure I locked up last night."

"I'm sure you did, too." Joyce narrowed her eyes. She could recall the exact moment that Brenda turned the key. Her stomach churned as she wondered what Jerry might have been up to.

Brenda could barely take a breath as her chest tightened.

"Maybe he's not dead, I hope he's not dead."

"Brenda, something terrible has happened here." Joyce couldn't find any words to reassure her. She didn't think there was any good explanation. As the police began to arrive, Joyce pulled Brenda away from the crowd.

"Brenda, I think he must have been here to sabotage our truck." She crossed her arms as she looked back at the body that was now surrounded by police officers, medical personnel and a few of Jerry's employees.

"You really think he would break in to try to cause our business some kind of harm?" Brenda frowned and looked away from the scene. "What a terrible man. But that doesn't mean that he deserved this."

"No, it doesn't. But it does make me wonder what he might have done." She shivered some as the possibilities raced through her mind. "He could have contaminated our supplies, or even planted something to make us fail a health inspection."

"Joyce!" Brenda narrowed her eyes as she looked back at her friend. "I hardly think this is the time to be focusing on that. Jerry is dead. What does it matter what he did to our truck?"

"What does it matter?" Joyce forced down a flash of anger. "It matters because, although this is a tragic moment, we don't deserve to lose our business either. It matters because whatever he did was the last thing he did in life, and perhaps it had something to do with his death. Most of all it matters because he died in our truck, and soon word will spread through the entire town. Which means that we will have to fight the rumors and the hit to our reputation in order to win customers back." She pursed her lips. "I'm surprised you're not more concerned about this."

"Well Joyce, I don't mean to sound harsh, but when someone dies my first thought isn't how it may affect me financially. I think about his family, and his friends, who will have to suffer his loss." She wrung her hands. "I don't even know if he was married. Do you?"

"I doubt that anyone could be married to a man like that." She gritted her teeth. "I understand where you're coming from, Brenda, and you're right, he probably had some family or friends that will miss him. But that doesn't mean that we should overlook the fact that he might have been here to destroy us, and if we aren't careful he will succeed at that, even though he's already gone."

"Yes, I guess you have a point." Brenda sighed. "We'll have to make sure we inspect things really well."

"Top to bottom. I want to know what he was up to."

~

It didn't take long before the police had control of the crowd. They roped off the area and shooed Joyce and Brenda back away from the truck.

Joyce paced back and forth, her breath puffing out into the air before her in quick white clouds. Brenda watched the paramedics and police surround Jerry. She noticed another man approach the scene. He was about Joyce's age, and wore a suit.

"Isn't that…" She paused a moment, then looked over at Joyce. "Detective Crackle is here."

"Detective Crackle?" She looked in the direction that Brenda pointed. "I didn't expect him to be here."

They'd met in less than ideal circumstances and knew that he was a homicide detective. Why would he be at the scene of a heart attack? An eerie feeling passed through her.

"Whatever happens next, the important thing is that we get the truck back up and running as soon as possible."

"I know why you feel that way, Joyce, but it's still hard for me to think about that right now." She frowned as she studied her friend. "He might not have been our favorite person, but he was still a person, and now he's gone."

"I know that, Brenda, I really do, and I am sorry that someone will be grieving him." Joyce shivered some as she watched Detective Crackle walk in their direction. "But you have to understand that his intentions were to stop us from succeeding and I do not want to allow that to happen. Even in death he might destroy us, so we have to be on top of things and ready to combat the rumors and issues we might face. It may seem callous to you, but it's not my intention to be. I just know that if we don't get ahead of this, we might not recover from it."

"Ladies." Detective Crackle paused in front of them. "I understand that you two had some interactions with the deceased?"

"Yes, we did." Joyce rested a hand lightly on Brenda's shoulder. "We spoke with him several times."

"As I understand it, there was some conflict?" He pulled out his notepad.

"Yes, but what does that have to do with anything?" Joyce tried to hide the defensiveness in her tone, but she could hear her words edged with it.

Detective Crackle must have heard it as well as he looked up at her sharply.

"I'm just trying to get an idea of the environment here at the market, what his last moments might have been like, and why he ended up in your food truck. Did he have a key?" His stern gaze lingered on Joyce a moment longer before he shifted his attention to Brenda.

"No, of course not." Brenda glanced over at

Joyce. She could tell that Joyce wanted to take the lead in the conversation with the detective, and she was a little concerned that she might say something she shouldn't.

"Then, what was he doing there?" He tapped his pen on the notepad and passed a glance between the two of them.

"It's not as if we invited him." Joyce frowned. "We were surprised to find him there. I mean, I think it's pretty clear that he broke in. Don't you?"

"No, it's not clear." He looked at the truck. "Do you have any cameras?"

"No." Brenda shook her head. "Well we do, but they aren't hooked up. They kept giving us trouble and losing the connection, so we just gave up on them for the moment. We are planning on getting them fixed."

"I see." He made a note and met her eyes. "If you'll excuse us, Brenda, I'd like to speak to Joyce alone." He did not look away from Joyce as he spoke.

"I think it's best if I stay with her, she's had quite a shock." Brenda slipped her hand into Joyce's.

"If you don't mind, I have a few questions to ask, and since Joyce is the owner of the truck, she is the one I'd like to speak with." He took a slight step back and held out his hands, with the notepad folded up in one. "Let me make it clear to you both, we can do this here, or we can do this at the station."

"What?" Joyce's stomach flipped. "What are you talking about? Why would we need to go down to the station? Because he had a heart attack?"

"What we have here, right now, is a suspicious death. There is no indication that it was a heart attack, and we won't know exactly what happened until some testing is done. However, Jerry was in very good health. Of course, there are still possible medical causes for his death, but the fact that you claim he may have broken into your truck indicates to me that there may be much more to this. I don't want to take you downtown to have these conversations, but if that is what it takes in order for me to get a little bit of cooperation, then that is what I will do." He looked into Joyce's eyes again, his gaze determined.

"Fine." She drew a slow breath and let the tension ease from her muscles. She certainly wasn't going to put Brenda in a position where she would be in the back of a police car. She could admit that she was being uncooperative, and it might have been for a few reasons. The main one would be the strange sensation she experienced when she was around the detective. She'd seen him around town quite a bit, and he had been to their donut truck at least once a week lately. That wasn't unusual, since many of the local police officers enjoyed the discount they offered to safety and rescue personnel.

"Joyce, are you sure?" Brenda frowned as she looked at the detective. "You have no reason to take us to the station, and I also know that you couldn't force us to go unless we were under arrest, and you certainly have nothing to arrest us for."

"You may be right about all of that." Detective Crackle nodded as he offered her a tight smile. "But after many years of experience in this job, I've discovered there is always a way to get around pesky rules and regulations. Would you like me to explain how?"

"Enough." Joyce gave Brenda's hand a squeeze. "I'll be fine. We're just going to have a conversation. It's not a big deal."

"All right, but if you need me just let me know." Brenda reluctantly released her hand. She wasn't sure if it was the right thing to walk away, but she knew that she didn't have another option. Once Joyce decided she wanted something a certain way, there was no changing her mind. As she stepped away from the pair, she noticed the way that Detective Crackle moved closer to Joyce. Most might assume it was an attempt to intimidate the petite woman, but she saw something else in it, as if it was protective. The thought hung in her mind as she walked over to a group of people that had gathered quite close to the truck. She knew there would be a lot of questions to answer, and the truth was she had just as many of her own. If what Detective Crackle indicated was true, maybe Jerry hadn't died from natural causes. Maybe there was more to it than that. Jerry had his share of enemies. Who would hate him enough to want to kill him? She hadn't seen a mark on him, how would someone kill him without leaving a mark?

CHAPTER 4

*O*nce Brenda walked away, Joyce felt a little uneasy alone with the detective. There wasn't a thing about him that she feared, but there was that strange ripple of familiarity, as if she had known him for some time. It confused her, as she didn't really know him that well at all.

"I appreciate you deciding to cooperate with me." He unfolded his notepad again and began to scribble something down on it. "Please understand my only goal here is to make sure I have as much information as early as possible, just in case this turns out to be more than a death investigation. I know I came on a little strong, I apologize for that. It's been a rough morning." He lifted his eyes from the notepad to hers.

"I'm not always the most pleasant myself." Joyce offered a half-smile. "How can I help?"

"About these disagreements you've had with Jerry, what was the main issue that led to them? Did you have a personal relationship with him?"

"No, I didn't have any kind of relationship with him. The main issue is that he was painful." She lifted her shoulders in a mild shrug. "I shouldn't say that, now that he's dead, right?" She grimaced. "But, it's the truth." She noticed that his expression grew tense once more, and wondered if she had been a little too honest.

"Being painful is rather subjective. Could you be a little more specific please?" He tapped his pencil against the notepad. Each strike of the eraser against the paper caused Joyce to feel even more irritated. Her mind filled with all of the things that Jerry could have sabotaged inside the truck. What if she had to replace everything? There was no money for that. They'd invested a lot in supplies to be ready for the market even though they hadn't all been delivered, and every minute the truck stayed closed, was a loss that would be harder to recover from.

"He didn't like it that the market gave us a slot

instead of his bakery and particularly a slot on the side of the market that was closer to his bakery. However, we had nothing to do with that, the market assigned all of the slots." She slid her hands into her pockets and did her best to calm herself down. "He was also not a very kind man. He liked to cause trouble with everyone he knew. I hate to say this, but I doubt that I was the only one he had a problem with. In fact, I know that many of his employees and other shop and truck owners had issues with him."

"Couldn't part of the situation have been resolved or at least appeased by you simply moving the truck? It is on wheels, isn't it?" He flashed her a grin that seemed completely inappropriate at that moment, and yet there was something remarkably endearing about it.

"No, we couldn't just move the truck, as it was the only slot available to us. If we tried to move it then we would risk being kicked out of the market. Plus, there was no reason for us to move it. We were fully within our rights to be there. He simply didn't like having the competition." She studied the detective for a moment. "What are all of these questions really about, Detective? I was married to a detective for many years and I have seen enough cop shows to know there's no reason to investigate a death from natural causes."

"You watch a lot of those shows, eh?" He lifted an eyebrow and his brown eyes flashed for a moment. "Then you should know I don't have to offer my reasoning to you. I like to be thorough on any case I investigate. There was clearly conflict here before this death occurred. I like to cover all of my bases."

"I'm sure that you do. However, I am quite shaken by all of this and I'd like to stop talking about it now." She slipped her hands back out of her pockets and crossed her arms.

"Shaken?" He reached out and rested his hand on the curve of her shoulder. His touch was warm, if not a little heavy and his expression seemed kind. "I doubt that anything could shake you, Joyce."

His words were so personal, so to the point, that her heart fluttered in response to them. They were also accurate. Not much did leave her shaken. But his touch, combined with the steadiness of his gaze, certainly left her flustered.

"I'm sure you wouldn't know if that was true or not. Regardless, am I free to go?" She brushed his hand from her shoulder and took a slight step back.

"Yes." He cleared his throat as his hand fell back

to his side. "You're welcome to go. But keep in mind that these moments are very important. Please try to remember any detail that might become important later, as I may need to speak with you again." As he started to turn away, she reached out and lightly touched his forearm. It was unusual for her to restrain someone this way, especially someone she didn't know well, but her mind was stuck on him, and her instincts told her there was more to the intensity of his investigation.

"Why do you think that?"

He turned back to face her, his cheeks slightly reddened as he studied her.

"I'm just doing my job, Joyce."

"It's more than that, isn't it?" She searched his eyes, and noticed the way they darkened with emotion as she pressed him for more information.

"You're quite the investigator yourself, aren't you?" He smiled some. "If you really want to know, yes, I have good reason to believe that this was not a death from natural causes. Jerry happened to be a good friend of mine, and I know for a fact that he was as healthy as a horse. So to find him like this, it's a shock to say the least, and one I'm going to thoroughly investigate." He met her eyes, again. "As I said, Joyce, I'll be in touch."

She was stunned by his confession. Suddenly, his abrupt attitude and harsh tone made a little more sense to her. He'd lost a friend, and he wanted to know why.

"Detective, I'm sorry for your loss." Her stomach twisted with guilt for the way she spoke about Jerry to him. "I'm sure there was another side to him, one I didn't have the chance to get to know."

"Not really." His lips curved beneath his bushy mustache into a wry smile. "But we were friends for some time, and at some point, the flaws everyone else sees, just fade away. He had his flaws, just like I do, but I doubt very much that he simply dropped dead. If someone did this to him, I'm going to find out who, no matter what it takes."

"I understand." Her heart dropped as she noticed the way he looked at her. Did he think she had something to do with it?

~

*A*s Brenda joined the crowd of people gathered near the truck, she could feel some stares from those around her. Most of them were familiar faces. She either knew them from town, or worked at the market with them. However, some of them she didn't recognize. She guessed they might be from the surrounding neighborhood and had just come out to see what all of the sirens and lights were about. It was still before seven in the morning, and so much activity so early was markedly unusual.

"Brenda, what happened?" A tall man who always had an eager smile under his graying mustache walked over to her.

"Donny, it looks like Jerry, the owner of the bakery, is dead. We found him when we arrived to open up this morning," she stumbled over her words as they felt so foreign to her. She wasn't sure how to explain what happened other than that, and yet the description seemed harsh.

"What?" His eyes widened behind his thin glasses. "Dead you say? Are you sure?"

"Yes." She sighed. "I'm afraid so."

"Dead?" Another man stepped closer to them. He was shorter, rounder, and nearly completely bald. "But how?"

"I'm not sure exactly, Chad." Brenda shuddered under the scrutiny as everyone in the crowd turned to look at her. She had expected they would have questions, but she didn't feel prepared to answer them, at least not all of them. "It looks like it might have been a heart attack. Or something like that."

"On your truck?" Donny looked past her towards the gathering of police officers outside the truck. "But why was he on your truck? Were you three fighting again?" He narrowed his eyes.

His words made her nerves buzz. Did everyone in the crowd know about their issues with Jerry?

"No, of course not. We didn't even speak with him this morning. We found him there when we arrived." She cleared her throat. "I'm not sure how he got in."

"Are you saying he broke in?" Chad sneered, and narrowed his eyes. "Are you saying he was committing a crime and ended up dead?"

"I'm not saying anything." She held up her hands and took a step back. The tone in the man's voice concerned her. Was he accusing her of something? "I'm just as confused as everyone else here. The police are investigating it, and I'm sure they'll get to the bottom of it. The important thing right now is to think about his family, and his friends, who have lost someone very dear to them."

"Family and friends?" A voice behind her scoffed. "I doubt that guy could even get affection from a dog." He chuckled.

She turned to see Clarence a few steps behind her. He folded his arms across his chest as he stared at her.

"Sometimes people aren't what they seem, Clarence." She lifted her shoulders in a mild shrug. "I'm sure he had someone that cared about him."

"Don't be so sure." Clarence pursed his lips. "I've never seen him with another person, other than Orville. Honestly, I thought Orville was the only person on earth that could get along with Jerry, but all of that changed a couple of days ago."

Brenda recalled hearing Jerry and Orville arguing the day before.

"Why was that?" She couldn't hold back her curiosity. Maybe if she knew a little bit more about Jerry's life, she wouldn't have such a sinking feeling in her gut. But for their few run-ins, Jerry was a stranger to her, and she wasn't sure how to feel about his death. She wanted to be sad, but instead she felt more confused than anything. Joyce was right, it appeared as if he was clearly trying to do something to the truck when he died. How could you feel much grief over his loss when it appeared as if the victim wanted to sabotage you?

"Jerry up and fired him. No warning, no write-ups, nothing. He didn't even give Orville the chance to defend himself or apologize." Clarence shook his head and rubbed his hand along the back of his neck. "It must have been humiliating for Orville."

"What was Jerry so upset about that he would do that?" She glanced back at Joyce and the detective. She wondered what kind of conversation they were having. From the body language she could see, it wasn't a good one. She turned her attention back to Clarence.

"He made the plans to set up the stall near your truck, and he was telling us about his intentions, how we had to work the stall, and make sure to try to distract customers from your truck. Orville warned him that it was a bad idea and that he could get in trouble for trying to cause issues during the market. He said that it went against their contract to remain open and be a part of the market. But Jerry didn't want to hear any of it. He blew up at Orville, I honestly thought he was going to deck the guy. Instead he fired him, in front of me and Mark, just like that. Orville has worked there since Jerry opened the bakery, but all it took was one disagreement and Orville was gone. That was the kind of man Jerry was, so please excuse me if I don't cry a river over the guy's death. It wouldn't surprise me at all if he broke into your truck to cause issues. I don't know what his problem with you and Joyce was, but it was a big one." The more he spoke the more animated he became, with a louder tone and hands flying through the air to illustrate his description. She guessed he was barely over eighteen, but he seemed mature for his age.

"I don't know either." She bit into her bottom lip. "But whatever it was, it wasn't mutual. All we wanted was to work in peace. I tried to work things out with him, but he didn't want to budge."

"Yeah, that was Jerry." Clarence shook his head. "I'm going to find Mark." He turned and strode away, just as Joyce headed towards the crowd. Brenda was eager to speak to her as she arrived.

"How did it go?"

"Not good." Joyce gritted her teeth, then met Brenda's eyes. "Apparently he was friends with Jerry. There I was saying bad things about him, without ever knowing that. Not only that, but he's pretty much convinced this wasn't natural causes."

"He is?" Brenda's heart lurched. "But that's ridiculous, there was no evidence of any injury."

"I know. I just can't fathom how Detective Crackle could be friends with a man like Jerry. I suppose if he was, then he might not be much better than Jerry himself." She crossed her arms.

"I don't know, he's always struck me as a very good detective. Maybe he's just upset because he has lost a friend. I hope that he will calm down soon." Brenda shivered as a cold breeze carried through the air and right down an opening in her scarf.

"Here comes Detective Crackle again, I wonder what he's going to have to say?" Joyce narrowed her eyes as he approached.

CHAPTER 5

All eyes turned to the detective as everyone waited to hear what might have happened to Jerry. Brenda suspected he wouldn't be able to tell them that, and yet there was still a hope within her that he would.

"Okay folks, I hate to tell you this, but the market is not going to run today. You're all going to have to clear out the area. Please be sure to see one of the police officers before you leave to give him or her your information, including your name, a phone number where we can reach you, and what your purpose was at the market today. I know that many of you rely on this market for your income, so this may be upsetting, but I can assure you that we will get it reopened as quickly as we possibly can."

After several groans and protests rippled through the crowd, Detective Crackle's mild tone became a little bit sterner.

"I have no option but to shut down the market while this matter is investigated. Keep in mind that a life was lost today, and it is my job to ensure that we know exactly what happened. I can't stress to you enough the importance of this. There will be officers available to answer any questions."

As the crowd began to disperse, Brenda and Joyce glanced at each other.

"Well, we thought this was going to be a good day." Brenda sighed.

"Yes, we did." Joyce pursed her lips. "I guess we'd better go check on things at the truck." She started to take a step towards it, but Detective Crackle moved in front of her before she could.

"Where are you going?" He crossed his arms.

Brenda frowned. She noticed the tension in his voice.

"We're going to make sure the truck is locked up. They've taken Jerry, haven't they?" Joyce noticed that the ambulance that had arrived, pulled away minutes before.

"Yes, they have, but that doesn't mean that you can go near the truck. As of now, it is a crime scene, and you will not be allowed back in it until it has been fully searched." He eyed Joyce for a moment, then looked towards Brenda. "I know this is an inconvenience, but I'm certain that you are interested in doing what's best for the investigation."

"What investigation?" Joyce's voice raised an octave. "There's nothing to investigate! He just died, Detective Crackle. I am very sorry for your loss, but how can you call it a crime scene when no crime has been committed?" Her cheeks flushed with frustration.

"This has nothing to do with Jerry being my friend. I am doing what I would do no matter who was found dead this morning. Please do not accuse me of doing anything other than my job." He quirked a brow in her direction. "It is a crime scene until the suspicious death has been ruled either natural causes, accidental, or a homicide. If you have a problem with that, you're welcome to contact the police chief. As of now, you are not allowed to enter that truck or even come within five hundred feet of it. Until I hear differently from the chief, or the matter is resolved, that is how it will stand. Understand?" He looked into Joyce's eyes. "That is not going to be a problem, is it?"

"Not going to be a problem?" She stepped

forward until she was toe to toe with the taller man. "You're going to rifle through our things, and keep us out of our own truck like common criminals, when Jerry died breaking into our truck. We have no idea what he might have been doing in there. Clearly his intentions were to sabotage it. So how can you act as if it is not a problem for us to be kept out of it?"

"Calm down." He gazed down at her, but did not take a step back. She could feel the pressure of his dark eyes as they probed through her own gaze. "I doubt that Jerry would have done anything to harm your truck, or either of you. But no matter what the reason is that he was there, his death investigation has to come first. I will let you know if we come across anything unusual inside the truck. You can fight me on this if you feel that's necessary, but please understand that it could lead you into a court battle that you would not win. Now, if you'll excuse me, I have to do my job." He stared at her a moment longer. "I'll keep you apprised of my findings."

"You can expect to hear from my lawyer, and the chief, when I get through with him!" Joyce looked back at Brenda, and in that moment the detective chose to walk away. Joyce turned back to find him gone, and her frustration grew even stronger. "How can he do this? How can he just take our truck?"

"Joyce, he didn't take it." Brenda spoke in a gentle voice in an attempt to calm her friend down. "He's holding it while they investigate. It's okay really. He's right, the important thing is to find out what happened to Jerry. If it wasn't natural causes, then of course we need to know what happened."

"How could it be anything but natural causes?" Joyce's anger faded some as that question rolled through her mind. "Do you think it was something else?"

"I don't know what to think at this point. But Jerry certainly had his share of enemies, and there are ways to kill a person without leaving a mark on them. So, yes, I guess, I'm curious about just how he died." She glanced around at the people who were shutting down their trucks and stalls. "Everyone here is impacted by what happened, we can't just pretend that it isn't a big deal. Jerry wasn't the greatest person, I know, but he's dead, and he deserves to have someone find out why."

"Yes, I suppose you're right about that." Joyce sighed as she wiped her hands along her pants. Her palms had gotten sweaty when she balled them into fists. "I get so wound up about things sometimes. It's easy for me to forget that the business isn't the number one priority. Life has to come first, or death in this case."

"Right." Brenda felt a little relieved as Joyce began to calm down. "I could never be as brave as you and stand up to him like that. Weren't you worried that he would arrest you?"

"Honestly, I didn't even consider it. Sometimes my temper gets away from me. But I've also learned over the years that you have to fight for what's important to you. You can't ever let it slip away, without at least struggling to hold on to it. I've had so many things taken." Her voice trailed off for a moment, then when she spoke again it was a little bit stronger. "But I will not let anyone take this from us, Brenda. Not ever." She turned to look at her friend. "You know that, don't you?"

"Yes, I know." She smiled some as she looked into Joyce's eyes. Their normally clear blue shade was clouded by the heaviness of the morning. As the time inched closer to eleven o'clock, she realized it had only been a few hours since they woke up that morning filled with enthusiasm for the day. How could so much change in such a short time? As difficult as it was to understand, there was no way to deny it. Jerry was dead, and until the detective was satisfied, they would not be allowed to re-open the truck.

"There's nothing more that we can do here. We should take his advice and head out." Brenda pulled Joyce away from the crowd of people who still had curious, and quite prying eyes on the crime scene. Those that weren't looking at it, had their attention focused on Joyce and Brenda. After the detective's decision that they couldn't enter 'Donuts on the Move' to close it up, they were looking at them with even more suspicion. It didn't matter what the truth was, once the rumors got started the damage to the reputation of their truck might be terrible. But again, there was nothing that they could do about that right then, and the best way to get Joyce to calm down was to get her home. However, as they approached the car she was already on the phone with the police chief.

"I'd like to know why you think you have the right to refuse to allow me on my property. That's right, I own it. It was broken into, and I want to make sure that nothing was taken or destroyed." Joyce paused as she heard the man on the other end of the phone draw a long breath.

"I will tell you right now that you are not going

to get into that truck until it is released from our custody. You can blow your horn, you can call your lawyer, but no one gets on that truck without my authorization. Given the fact that your late husband was a detective I would expect you to understand that we are just doing our job. I can assure you that if there is anything damaged you will be informed."

"And how can I just trust that the police officers aren't going to do further damage? How will I know what Jerry might have done, and what your officers might have done, or what that detective might plant in there to make me look bad. He really does not like me, you know?"

"I can't imagine why." He coughed. "I mean, perhaps if you calmed down and treated him with a bit more respect, you would recognize that he does not have a vendetta, he is only trying to do his job, which you seem to be quite determined to prevent him from doing. There are two sides to every coin, you know."

"Oh yes, I do know that. And, if my truck isn't released to me by tomorrow morning, I will make sure that you see both sides of my lawyer." With that she hung up the phone.

Brenda cringed as she climbed into the car. She

admired Joyce's ability to be confrontational, but sometimes she worried that she took it a little too far.

"Joyce, maybe take it easy on the lawyer talk." She frowned as she started the car.

"Why should I?" She looked at her with some annoyance and leftover aggression. "What they're doing is wrong. Can't you see that? Do you have any idea how much money we're going to lose over this?"

"Is it wrong, though?" She looked over at her friend. "They do have to investigate Jerry's death, and as unnerving as it is for us to have to wait until they are done to find out what happened inside the truck, it's still for the best, for the investigation."

"But that's what I don't understand. I'm not so sure that there really needs to be an investigation. I can't imagine that anyone killed Jerry, despite his bad attitude." Joyce shook her head as she stared hard out the window. "The problem is Detective Crackle. If he didn't know Jerry personally, he might just think that this was a death from natural causes. Instead, he is going to turn over every rock until he is certain that if his friend was killed the murder is solved."

"Which is understandable and maybe a good thing." Brenda tipped her head from side to side. "I would do that, too, if something happened to a friend of mine."

"Honestly, I don't even want to think about it anymore. I just want it to be over with." Joyce curled her hands tightly together in her lap.

For the first time Brenda realized that all of this anger Joyce was experiencing had more to do with anxiety than fury. She'd been just as frightened by Jerry's death, as Brenda, maybe even more so. She reached out and patted Joyce's knee.

"I know it was scary to see him like that, and I know it's frightening to lose control over who is in the truck. But there is one thing I'd like you to consider." She turned down the street that led to Joyce's house.

"What is it?" Joyce felt a bit calmer after Brenda's reassurance. She always seemed to be able to reach her, even when she was a bit frantic.

"Suppose this does turn out to be a homicide, suppose that someone really did kill him, in our truck. What do you think that will make us?" She glanced over at Joyce.

"Wait, are you saying that they will suspect that

we had something to do with this?" Joyce's eyes widened as the idea dawned on her for the first time.

"I would, wouldn't you? We had run-ins with him, he died in our truck, and we've made no secret of our dislike for the man." She frowned. "Honestly, I think we'd be prime suspects. And if we are, I can't imagine that it will help us any if we have already alienated the detective on the case, as well as the police chief. At that point, the ball will be in their court as to how to treat us, and I imagine that people are less likely to want to throw you in jail if you are kind to them."

"And I've already upset them both." Joyce sighed as she closed her eyes. "I get the point, Brenda, and I'm sorry. But I'm sure it won't come to that. After all, we both saw Jerry, it sure didn't look like someone had killed him." She tried to believe her own words, but as the car turned into her driveway she felt more than the bump of the uneven pavement. She was jostled from the inside by the possibility that this really could turn into a murder investigation. One that could put both herself and Brenda at risk of being arrested.

Brenda was silent as she turned off the car. Her mind churned with all of the possibilities. Though

Joyce seemed to think that there wasn't any danger of this turning into a homicide investigation, she wasn't so sure. She knew that Jerry had angered a lot of people, and sometimes people did the unthinkable. However, why would it happen in their truck? How did it happen, if he didn't have any visible injuries? She guessed that it would have had to be planned ahead of time. She glanced at the time on her phone as she stepped out of her car. Sophie would be out with her parents for a day of Christmas activities. Charlie would be hard at work on yet another article. All she could think about was just how many hours there were left between the time when Jerry's death was just suspicious, and when the truth came out. If it was natural causes, their lives would soon go back to normal, but if it was something more, things would become far different.

"Are you okay, Brenda?" Joyce looked over at her as she unlocked the front door.

"I think so. I'm just going to make a call to Charlie. I'll be right in." She smiled at Joyce, but her heart wasn't in it. Once she was alone outside, she dialed her husband's number. It rang several times, then went to voicemail. As she left a rambling message about everything that happened, she wondered if he would even listen to it. He had a bad habit of deleting voicemails without playing the message. When she hung up, her stomach was in knots. She wanted to hear his voice, and most of all she wanted to know that everything would be okay.

CHAPTER 6

*W*hen Brenda stepped inside, she found Joyce in the kitchen putting together a snack for them.

"I don't know if you can eat or not, but I'm a nervous eater. I eat when I'm nervous." She poured crackers onto a plate and followed it with slices of cheese. "Were you able to reach him?"

"I'm a nervous eater, too." She grabbed a slice of cheese. "And no. He didn't answer. He's under deadlines, and I'm sure he will get back to me as soon as he gets a break. Honestly, there's not much that he can do even when he calls back. I just wanted to hear his voice."

"I understand. That's how I always felt about Davey. He would be on a case for days sometimes.

He was so focused on his work that sometimes I felt forgotten. But the moment I heard his voice, I could hear his love for me in it, and I knew that no matter what, he would never forget me." She smiled to herself. "I still feel that way, even though that may seem silly."

"It isn't silly to me." She patted the back of her hand. "I think it's a rare gift to find love like that. I'm so grateful for Charlie."

"And I'm sure he's grateful for you, too." Joyce pushed the plate towards the bar stools on the other side of the island. "Let's try to relax a little bit. We had a very rough morning."

"Yes, we did." The image of Jerry's body flashed through her mind. "I just can't stop thinking about it, though. How did he end up there?"

"He had to have broken in. There's no other explanation. Which means he had bad intentions." She plucked a cracker and slice of cheese off the plate.

"Maybe. But the door wasn't damaged. It was open. I know I locked it, I know it." Brenda frowned. "But maybe somehow I forgot?"

"No darling, you didn't. I saw you lock it with my own eyes. I know you locked it, too. Maybe he picked it or, maybe..." Joyce gasped, then her eyes widened. "Remember on Monday last week, when we first arrived at the market? We went in to the bakery to introduce ourselves and give them some donuts. I left my purse on the counter as Orville showed us around the bakery. When we returned I remember the flap on my purse being open. I was nervous, because I thought that someone had stolen my wallet, but everything was there."

"Okay?" Brenda studied her. "Why does that matter?"

"Because I never checked for the spare key. It's always tucked into the zippered part of my purse. I never use it, so I didn't even think to check for it." She hurried over to her purse which was on the table near the front door. As she rummaged through it, her heart pounded. If the key wasn't there, she would know that Jerry had taken it. After a second thorough search, she nodded. "That's it. It's gone. How could I be so stupid?"

"Joyce, there is nothing stupid about you." She joined her at the table. "Are you sure it isn't in there? Maybe it slipped into the lining?"

"No, it's just not there. I've looked twice. There are no holes in the lining. Which means he took it, or someone else in that bakery did." Joyce narrowed her eyes.

"Jerry wasn't there when we arrived, as far as we know, but he was there when we left. But Matt, Clarence, and Orville were there, too." She shook her head. "I can't believe he did this. He took the key to the truck? That means he could have been in it any time he wanted to. What a creep!" She frowned. "I'm starting to think that you're right, Joyce, maybe there wasn't a shred of decency in that man."

"Maybe not, but I can tell you this much for certain. He took that key to break into the truck, and find a way to destroy us. But was he alone? Maybe someone else took the key? Maybe he has a partner? We have to be very careful about who we trust from here on out. I can't believe how reckless I was by leaving my purse like that."

"It was a mistake that anyone could have made. Don't be so hard on yourself, Joyce."

"I'm trying not to be. But all I can think about is losing that truck. I know that would be horrible for both of us." Joyce slammed her purse down on the table. "If only that man had an ounce of decency we wouldn't be in this position right now."

"It's a lot to take in, but there really is no one but

himself to blame. Maybe he realized he was doing something wrong and panicked. Or maybe he thought he was going to be caught. Or maybe it was just his time and he happened to be in our truck. But honestly, trying to come up with a reason is going to drive us both crazy. I say we find a way to enjoy our afternoon together, put all of this as far out of our minds as we can."

"I know just the thing." Joyce snapped her fingers. "Music, and cocktails!"

"Cocktails?" Brenda started to decline, then she recalled that her daughter was safe and well taken care of with her parents. She didn't have to deny herself a little fun. "That sounds perfect."

Joyce cranked the music up, and soon the house was filled with lively Motown style music that Brenda couldn't resist dancing to. It was a much needed release for both of them. By the time they collapsed on the couch it was early evening, and Brenda recognized for the first time just how exhausted she was.

"Thanks, Joyce, that was exactly what I needed."

"It works for me every time." She laughed. "Davey is the one who taught me to do it, though.

My husband, the serious cop. The first time I saw him do it I thought he'd lost his mind."

"Really?" Brenda smiled at the thought of Joyce walking in on her serious husband in the middle of a dance fest.

"He had the music blasting, and he was dancing like a fool. No rhythm, just hopping around like an out of control kangaroo. I thought, this was it, he'd finally cracked. When he saw me, he was so embarrassed. I just asked him, what are you doing, honey? He explained to me that when he had a very tough case, he would dance it out. He said it was the only way to clear his head. Of course, I understood what he meant, it was about surrounding himself with levity. And when he came home and turned on the music, I would dance with him, to try to help him forget. Ever since, I've danced whenever there is something on my mind that I can't break free from. It gives you some freedom. It doesn't always make all of it disappear, but it at least gives you a chance to be without it for a short time."

"It definitely worked for me." Brenda laughed as Molly hopped up into her lap. "It looks like Molly had a good time, too." The bunny gazed up at her with a steady stare that made her wonder just what she was thinking.

"She knows you need some company. I'll let her stay with you tonight." She stretched her arms above her head. "I think after a quick dinner, I'm going to be ready to pass out. What about you?"

"Yes, I think so, too."

Brenda made a delicious meal for them, while Joyce kept her company, then they shared the meal at the table. Joyce dropped a few slices of carrot on Molly's mat on the floor for her to gobble up. The bunny was a bit of a beggar, and Brenda had never seen anything cuter. She had a brief conversation with Sophie after dinner, that consisted of her recounting the amazing day she had and how much fun her grandparents were. It was good to hear her voice, and reminded her that she had a lot of positive things in her life to focus on. She couldn't wait to see her at Christmas. As rough as the day had been, she had managed to find some peace thanks to a wonderful friend, and the infectious giggle of her six-year-old.

"How is Sophie?" Joyce smiled at her as she hung up the phone.

"Good, she's really good."

"I'm glad. I'm ready for bed." She yawned, then shivered. "I guess we don't have to get up early tomorrow."

"You're right." She gave Joyce a warm hug. "Thanks for being such an amazing friend, Joyce."

"Thank you, too." She smiled. "I'll see you in the morning. Molly will be good company." She reached down and gave the bunny a light stroke on her back. Then she scooped her up and handed her over to Brenda. "Trust me, she's better than a teddy bear."

"I'm sure she is. She's certainly softer." Brenda ran her fingers through the bunny's fur. "Good night, Joyce. Tomorrow will be better."

"Good night, Brenda, I sure hope so." She headed off to her room.

$\sim$

After Joyce closed her door, Brenda snuggled with Molly a little bit longer. She was a cuddly bunny, and the animal seemed to sense that Brenda needed a little extra comfort. Her mind swirled with everything she and Joyce discussed. She hoped that she was wrong, and Detective Crackle didn't really have something against them that could impact them in the long run. She was not yet willing to believe that their lives were going to be changed by becoming the main suspects of a murder investigation.

To calm her thoughts Brenda focused on the idea that Jerry had died of natural causes and that the investigation would prove just that. It might take a little time for them to be sure, but once they were, they would be able to move on from all of this and return to the excitement they once felt about the market, and the holidays in general. She was looking forward to seeing Sophie again when she came back home to join her parents for Christmas, and was glad that she invited Joyce to join them as her kids were grown up and were away. Brenda hated the thought of Joyce being alone on Christmas, but she also knew that it would be up to Joyce if she preferred it.

Another thing Brenda admired about Joyce was how comfortable she seemed to be on her own. Sometimes the thought crossed her mind that Charlie might walk away, or something terrible could happen to him, and the idea of being without him was horrible enough, but even just the mundane thoughts of what she would do if she was single, overwhelmed her. She'd become so used to having a partner that she couldn't imagine what it would be like without one. However, she did know that she would find a way to handle it for the sake of her daughter.

"Oh, now my mind is really running away. I've got to get some sleep." She gave the bunny another stroke, then set her free on the floor to run around. As she stood up to head to bed in the guest room, her cell phone began to ring. She picked it up quickly, hoping that the sound wouldn't wake Joyce.

"Hello?" She answered in a whisper.

"Brenda, are you okay?"

She smiled at the sound of her husband's voice. As she sank down on the couch she closed her eyes.

"I'm so glad to hear from you, Charlie, you will not believe the day I had."

"I got your message, and immediately started looking into things. I'm sorry I'm not there with you, sweetheart."

"It's okay, I know you're busy. It was horrible, but I'm just glad it will all be over soon."

"Maybe not as soon as you think, I'm afraid."

Her eyes popped open. "What do you mean?"

"Are you sitting down?"

"Uh, yes?" She glanced at the couch that surrounded her. "Why?"

"Because I've just had some news that I think will be a bit shocking for you."

"What is it, Charlie?" She sat forward on the

couch and held her breath. She knew that if he was framing it so carefully it had to be something very serious.

"According to a friend of mine that does reporting on local crimes, Jerry did not die of natural causes. When his body was examined they detected a substance on his lips and teeth that they suspect is poison. They are running tests to confirm that it is poison and exactly what type of poison it is. They also need to determine if he actually ingested it. But at the moment they are treating this as a suspicious death."

"Oh no!" She gasped and stood up from the couch. "This can't be happening! I didn't want to think it was possible. But how would someone get him to eat poison? I mean, that is just awful. Wouldn't he have tasted it? Wouldn't he have fought back?"

"Not if it was in a food or drink, more than likely a food, since there were bits of it remaining on his teeth and lips. I would say someone made him some-thing that contained the poison, and he ate it. If it had a foul taste it might have been able to be disguised with strong flavor or sugar. Sweetheart, do you understand what this means?" His voice grew even more tense.

"Yes, I think I do." Her heart dropped. "It means that we're going to be looked at as suspects in his death. It means that someone murdered him, in our truck. Maybe even someone we know. Oh Charlie."

"It's okay, sweetheart, take a breath. Even if you are suspects it will only be for a brief time. You will be cleared quickly, I'm sure. But I'm sure the police will want to speak with you. You need to pay attention to what you say and use caution. Tomorrow morning we'll call a lawyer, and we can go into the station together for you to have an interview."

"Oh Charlie, you can't do that, I know how busy you are." Her heart fluttered with fear.

"It's all right, I'm not going to let you go through this on your own. I'm here for you."

His words reminded her of her thoughts about being alone. Who would be there to help Joyce? She wouldn't have anyone to call a lawyer for her, or walk her into the station. She would be able to handle things on her own.

"No Charlie, really. I love you, and I appreciate you wanting to offer me support, but I can handle this on my own. I promise. If something comes up I will call you right away. But like you said, this is simple, it will be cleared up quickly. There's no reason for you to lose any time at work."

"Are you sure?" He sighed. "I don't know about this. I'm very concerned."

"I know, so am I, but I will be fine. I love you, Charlie, and I can't wait to see you. But your work is important, and if you get behind then we might not be able to have the Christmas we hoped for, all together, relaxing, and nobody working. Remember last year?"

"Yes," he grumbled. "I missed my deadline and had to work through Christmas morning and dinner. I know, I know. I felt awful for ruining the day for us."

"You didn't ruin the day for us, silly." She smiled some as she recalled how wonderful he had been. "Sophie was sick, really sick, and I'd been up with her for three days straight. You had your deadline, but I was so exhausted that I couldn't stay awake, and so you took over for me. You stayed up with her all night and tried to write at the same time, but it didn't work out. You gave your all for our family, Charlie, and I can do the same, if you give me the chance. I want our Christmas to be relaxing and enjoyable for all of us this year, and that means you having the time to get your work done, and me handling this on my own is the best way that we can make sure that happens. So don't fight me on it, I'm perfectly capable of handling it."

"I know you are. I really do. I just hate that you have to deal with it on your own. If anything comes up, anything at all, I want to be the first number you dial. Got it?"

"Yes." She smiled at his words. "I'll make sure."

"I'm going to try to get some time to meet up with you tomorrow night. I need to see you."

"All right, we'll make sure that happens. For now, you focus on your stories, and I'll focus on getting some sleep. Okay?"

"I love you, Bren."

"I love you, too." As she hung up the phone she discovered that she didn't feel quite as confident as she implied over the phone. In fact, she was scared. What if she couldn't handle hiring a lawyer and going into the station? What if she did or said something wrong that somehow made her more of a suspect? She hoped that wouldn't be the case, but she knew it could always be a possibility. She hadn't exactly been accused of a crime before. She considered waking Joyce to tell her the news, but she decided to let her sleep instead. In the morning there would be a lot to face, at least she deserved one more peaceful night's sleep. As she crawled into bed, her stomach twisted and turned with dread. Now that she knew that it wasn't simply Jerry's time, as everyone's time came eventually, this had just become a whole lot more serious.

CHAPTER 7

Joyce's eyes fluttered open slowly. It was hard for her to recall exactly why she was annoyed, but she knew for certain she was. In fact, she was more than annoyed, she was upset. As the memory of the day before began to filter back through her mind, she realized it was because her truck was locked up, and Detective Crackle had proven to be an extremely difficult man. Since she didn't have to be up early to open up the truck she considered staying in bed for a few minutes. She had nothing pressing to deal with, other than trying to mend fences with the detective in order to put Brenda's mind at ease. However, she soon heard the clanging of dishes in the kitchen and could smell the scent of coffee in the air. Brenda was up, and she was preparing some breakfast, more than likely for both of them.

After a quiet groan into her pillow she pulled herself up out of bed. There were a few more aches and pains in her body than there used to be, but they were usually eased by her new tradition of performing yoga. That morning, she simply wasn't in the mood. Instead she wanted to grab a cup of coffee, eat whatever delicious food Brenda was making, and enjoy a quiet morning together with the woman she considered to be her close friend. As she passed the window in her room she noticed that the sky was quite gray. The weathermen had been falling all over themselves trying to predict when the first snow would be. It was embarrassing to watch, as each day they squeaked out their predictions, only to have them proven wrong. She looked forward to a bit of snow, but preferred nothing more than a dusting. On her way into the kitchen she checked on the laundry she'd done the night before. There would be clothes to fold, but they could wait. When she reached the kitchen she was greeted by the most delicious scent.

"Oh, you made cinnamon sugar donuts, didn't you?" Her mouth watered as Brenda turned to face her.

"Yes, I did." She smiled, but her smile faltered.

"Mm, thank you so much. That is just what I need this morning." She sat down on one of the bar stools at the kitchen island. "So, what had you up so early and baking?"

"There's something I need to tell you, Joyce, something very serious." She set one of the donuts on a plate and put it in front of Joyce. "Maybe you should have some coffee first."

"No, what is it?" Her mind became sharp as she sensed the urgency in Brenda's voice. "What's happened?"

"I spoke to Charlie last night. He got some information from a crime reporter, about Jerry's death." She braced herself for Joyce's reaction.

"What information? Out with it, girl! You're scaring me." Joyce's eyes widened. What could it possibly be? That he did not die of natural causes? She hoped that was not the case.

"He was poisoned." Brenda's eyes widened.

"What? He must be pulling your leg. Poison takes days to identify. I'm sure it's some kind of mistake." Her heart began to pound faster. It had to be a mistake. There was no other explanation for what happened.

"No, it's no mistake. Charlie said that Jerry still

had some of the food on his teeth and lips and from what they could identify they believe it was poisoned. They are just waiting for confirmation." She swallowed hard. "I have no idea what to think, but Charlie was certain the police would want to speak with us. He said I should hire a lawyer and go into the station to speak with the detective. I've already started making some calls this morning, but none of the offices are open yet."

"A lawyer, yes." Her head spun as the new information began to settle in. "Brenda, you should have told me this as soon as you knew! Where's my phone? I need to call my lawyer right this second." She stood up from the bar stool and tied her robe tighter around her body. Her muscles were tense as she thought of where this information might lead.

"I know I should have told you, but I didn't want to wake you. I figured we'd have time to handle everything this morning. I'll pour you some coffee." She reached for the coffee pot just as there was a loud knock on the front door.

Both women froze. In that moment they were thinking the same thing.

"Who could that be?" Joyce's throat grew dry as she spoke. She knew exactly who it would be.

The knock came again, louder this time. Joyce

knew that anything she did to hinder the investigation from this point on would only make her look more guilty. If it was the police there to arrest her and she didn't open the door, then they would consider her uncooperative.

"Joyce, maybe you should answer." Brenda squeezed her hands together in a tight knot. "I don't think they're just going to go away. It can't be the police. Charlie said I could just walk in with a lawyer and…"

"And he didn't take Detective Crackle into account. That man is like a pit bull with a raw steak." She grimaced at her own imagery and walked hesitantly to the door. As she reached up to smooth out her hair and adjust the collar of her robe, she realized that it would be the first time a man had seen her in her robe, since her husband had passed away. It was not exactly revealing, but that wasn't the point. It still felt inappropriate. Just before she reached for the knob, the person outside knocked again, so hard that she jumped in reaction to the sound. Annoyed, she jerked the door open and stared into a pair of familiar brown eyes.

"Detective."

"Joyce." He took a step forward before she could close the door. "I need to speak with you. And you as well." He looked past her, to where Brenda stood a few steps behind Joyce.

"All right, come in." Joyce stepped back and held the door open for him.

"Thank you." He swept his gaze around the house briefly, then looked back to Joyce. "As I suspected, Jerry's death was a homicide. We have evidence that supports that."

"I'm very sorry to hear that." Joyce wrapped her arms around her robe to hold it shut even though the sash was already doing a very good job.

"As was I." He looked between the two of them. "I'm hoping that you can help me figure out exactly what happened here."

"Anything we can do to help, we're more than happy to," Brenda stammered out her words. She was nervous about speaking to him without the lawyer that Charlie had advised.

"Great. You can start by telling me where you were, the night before yesterday." He pulled out his notepad.

"We were here." Joyce gestured to the living room. "Right in there."

"Alone?" He made a note.

"Yes, alone." She frowned. "Well, we were here together, but alone."

"I understand." He turned his attention to Brenda. "Did you see anyone else, or speak to anyone? Did you order food or anything?"

"No, we just hung out." Brenda frowned. "We had dinner here. I cooked."

"I can see why. That smells delicious." He nodded towards the kitchen.

"Thank you." She lowered her eyes.

"So, what you're telling me is that neither of you have an alibi after you left the donut truck the night before Jerry died and when you arrived the following morning?" He made another note.

"We don't need an alibi, Detective. We had nothing to do with his death." Joyce frowned. "I know that you are grieving the loss of your friend, and you want to find answers, but we're not going to be able to provide any."

"Maybe you can." He tapped the eraser of his pencil against the notepad. "After some analysis we believe that Jerry was poisoned. The poison was a white powder that was found amongst some glaze. Not unlike the glaze that is used on a donut." He raised an eyebrow. "Do you two know anything about that?"

"No, of course not." Brenda bit into her bottom lip.

"Not at all. How could we?" Joyce sighed. "What a shame. I hope you figure out what happened to him, Detective, I really do."

"Here, would you like a cinnamon donut?" Brenda hurried to the kitchen and returned with a plate full of them. "Take a few."

"Uh, no thanks." He eyed the donuts as if he would devour the entire plate given the chance, but still shook his head. "I'll be in touch, ladies." He turned and walked out of the house. Joyce hurried to close the door behind him.

"Lock it." Brenda grabbed at the counter of the island as she watched Joyce turn the lock on the door.

"It's all right, Brenda, he's gone now." Joyce turned back to face her.

"I'm sorry, I'm so spooked. Did you see the way he refused the donuts? He must have thought they were poisoned! I am so worried now." She bit into her bottom lip. She was sure that a woman as strong as Joyce couldn't understand why she would be so frightened by the detective's visit.

"I'm also worried." Joyce walked towards her. Though she claimed to be scared, her stride was strong, and her narrowed eyes were sharp as ever. "I can't believe he had the nerve to walk into my home, and speak to me like that. I'll tell you this, right now, he's going to learn who exactly he is dealing with. I am not backing down on this. Not one bit."

"I believe you." She chewed on her lip as her heart raced. "But like he said, we don't have any alibi other than each other. That doesn't exactly bode well for us. I mean, everyone knows that we had trouble with Jerry, more than trouble. We came close to calling the police on him. So, him being found dead in our truck is just going to make people believe that we were definitely involved. And if people believe that, then what is to stop the police from believing that? I mean really, Joyce, we could end up in prison for this for the rest of our lives. I'll never get to see Sophie grow up, and poor Charlie will have to be a single parent. I mean, I'm sure he could handle it, but how awful is it that he will have to? And how am I going to handle being in prison? It's not as if I am tough, or strong, in any way. I mean, I don't think I'm going to survive it. I know it'll kill me to be away from Sophie and..."

"Brenda!" Joyce clapped her hands sharply and looked straight into her eyes. "Listen, take a breath. You're getting way too far ahead of yourself. We're not going to prison, that's not going to happen."

"How do you know that?" Brenda wiped at her

eyes. "I already messed this up, I never should have waited to tell you about this. If I'd woken you up last night, we could have made a plan, and maybe even fled the state and..."

"Brenda." Joyce put her hands on her shoulders. "No, you didn't do anything wrong. Okay? You have to calm down. You are stronger and tougher than you think, but panic is not going to do us any good right now. We have to push through this, and make the right choices. You need to have a clear head to do that."

"I don't think I can." Tears filled her eyes as she looked back at Joyce. "I just want to run, I don't think I can handle this."

"Yes, you can." She tightened her grasp on her shoulders. "You have to. You don't want to lose Sophie, do you?"

"No, no absolutely not." She closed her eyes to hold back fresh tears. "I'll do absolutely anything not to lose her."

"Okay, the first step is to calm down. Breathe with me, all right?" She took a long, slow breath.

"I'll try." She breathed in as slowly as she could. Only then did she notice just how fast she had been breathing. Joyce was right, she had been panicking. "I'm sorry." She breathed in again, and a few more times, before her heart finally began to settle.

"You have nothing to apologize for. It's normal to be frightened when someone barges in and accuses you of a crime you didn't commit. But we have to keep our wits about us. Detective Crackle is not one to back down. The important thing is that we have the truth on our side. We are innocent, we had nothing to do with Jerry's death."

"Yes, I know. But, the police don't know that. And, I've seen so many stories about innocent people being convicted of murder. I just don't want to be one of them." She took another breath.

"I know, I don't either. So, we can't just sit here and wait for it to happen. Our best defense is a good offense." She smiled as she pulled her hands away from Brenda's shoulders and began to pace through the kitchen.

"That sounds good, but what exactly does it mean?" She tilted her head to the side as she studied Joyce, who seemed cat-like in her movements.

"What it means is, we need to find out who actually killed Jerry. It's the only way to make sure that we don't become victims in this. As long as we find the real killer, Detective Crackle can't put us behind bars, no matter how much he may want to."

"You're right. That's perfect." Brenda nodded, relieved to have a goal to focus on. "But how are we going to do that? I mean, I have no idea who killed Jerry. Do you?"

"No. But I have some suspects in mind." Joyce raised an eyebrow.

"You do? Who?" Brenda joined her as she headed for the couch.

"I think Orville would be one. He was fired by Jerry recently, right?" She sat down on the couch.

"Yes, it was very messy. He could definitely have motive to kill Jerry." She pulled out her phone and began to make a list on it. "And maybe the other employees that work there?"

"Yes, they are a possibility, too. I think the more questions we ask, the more suspects will surface. We're going to have to get to know Jerry very well. Who his family was, who his friends were."

"Detective Crackle is one of them, right?" Brenda scrunched up her nose. "I can't see the two of them hanging out together."

"Oh, I can. After I saw the way he treated us today." She rolled her eyes. "But that does mean that Jerry is capable of friendship, which means he might have had other friends. It could have been a family member, too. Maybe someone finally snapped."

"Yes, but keep in mind, where he died. It was on our truck. I can't help but think someone was trying to send us a message."

"It's possible. But who would want to send us a message like that?" Joyce cringed. "I don't think anyone I know would want to do that. What about you? Do you have some skeletons in your closet that would warrant this?"

"No. Not that I know of anyway." She shook her head. "I guess you're right, it would be a bit of a stretch to believe that someone intentionally killed him and left him there. Unless, maybe the killer was trying to frame us?" Her eyes widened. "That's possible, isn't it?"

"Yes. But it could also have been a crime of convenience. If he was poisoned, it could have been slow-acting, and he just happened to be there when he died. Or the killer might have come upon him there, and given him the poison, so that is where he died." She tapped her chin lightly with a fingertip. "Yes, I think that could be a possibility."

"Oh, no, I just thought of something!" Brenda clasped a hand over her mouth.

"What, what is it?" Joyce scooted closer to her on the couch.

"Remember what we saw when we first arrived at the truck? Before we found Jerry?" She closed her eyes as she recalled the moment. "There were broken eggs all over the ground."

"Oh, my goodness, yes there were." She sat forward. "Do you think that Aaron might have something to do with it? Why would he want Jerry dead?"

"I don't know, but I don't think we can rule him out as a possibility. He was obviously there. Why else would the eggs be broken?" Brenda frowned.

"Unless Jerry broke those on his way into the truck. Aaron usually leaves them on the step up into the truck. So, maybe Jerry didn't see them, and stepped on them?"

"It's possible." Brenda rested her head back on the couch as she considered it. "But, I think we need to talk to Aaron. If he was there, he might have seen something."

"True. I wonder if anyone else was around that morning?" Joyce pursed her lips. "I'm pretty sure we were one of the first ones to arrive."

"I remember Gray mentioned that he came in at about five-thirty every morning. He might have been there, but I don't remember seeing him that morning. Of course, in all of the chaos, I might have just overlooked him. He did mention to me that he wasn't getting along with many of the other vendors. So maybe he would be a good resource to find out what might have been happening behind the scenes." She sighed. "At least we have an idea of where to start, though I'm not sure where it's going to lead."

"I'm not sure either." Joyce closed her eyes. "But we have to work through this together, Brenda. We're going to figure this out, I promise."

"I'm sure we will." She nodded. They looked at each other with a sense of determination. They were going to solve the murder.

CHAPTER 8

*O*ver the next few hours Brenda and Joyce pored over the list of vendors who worked at the holiday market. They went through each vendor and added the names of the people who they knew worked there. It was a long list, and didn't account for those that they didn't know or couldn't recall. It also didn't include those that delivered goods to the trucks and local stores. As they began to delve into adding those names to the lists, the number continued to creep up.

"Ugh, this seems impossible." Joyce pushed her tablet aside and closed her eyes. "There are just so many people that could have had access to Jerry, and the truck."

"Maybe we're coming at this the wrong way?"

Brenda drummed her fingers on the table. "We know that Jerry was there, right?"

"Of course." Joyce narrowed her eyes. "But how does that help?"

"Well, if he was there then he might have gone to the bakery. Maybe if we can get the footage from the bakery, we'll be able to see if he was there with anyone else. I'm sure the police have checked it, but it may help us to narrow down our suspects. What do you think?" She frowned.

"I think it's a great idea, but how are we going to get access to the recording? It's not as if the police will just hand it to us." Joyce rested her chin on her hand. "I could try asking Detective Crackle, but I'm fairly certain he would be less than inclined to offer me any help."

"No, but I might be able to get in contact with someone who would. Let me make a phone call." She grabbed her phone and stepped into the guest bedroom. As she dialed Charlie's number, her heart pounded. She could only imagine how anxious he was about the situation, and knowing she was looking into things would probably make him even more nervous.

"Hi sweetheart." His voice echoed through the phone. It was heavy with exhaustion.

"Oh Charlie, are you all right? Have you been sleeping at all?"

"I'm fine, don't worry about me. I'm just glad to hear your voice."

"Me too." She sighed and savored the connection with him for a moment. "Listen, does Richard still work in the video editing department?"

"Yes. Why?"

"Do you have his number? I need to ask him for a favor."

"What kind of favor, Brenda?" His voice grew more alert.

"I just want to see if he can get me a look at some security camera footage from the bakery." She held her breath as she wondered if he would refuse to give her the phone number.

"Yes, I'm sure he would." He paused a moment, then cleared his throat. "Do you think there's something on there that can clear you and Joyce?"

"I hope so."

"Here's the number." He rattled it off as she typed it into her phone. "Listen, I may be busy, but I'm here. So anything you need just let me know. Be careful about stepping on any toes in the police department, all right?"

"I'll do my best. Thanks for your help, Charlie. I hope you're able to get some rest soon."

"Soon. I love you."

"I love you, too." She hung up the phone. For a moment, her mind dwelled on how hard he worked, but the intensity of being a suspect in a murder investigation steered her focus back to Richard. She dialed his number.

"Richard Kessen."

"Hi Richard, this is Brenda, Charlie's wife?"

"I remember you, Brenda." His tone sounded friendly. "How are you holding up?"

She cringed as she realized that he probably knew every detail about Detective Crackle's suspicion of her.

"I'm doing okay, thanks. But I need a favor."

"All right, I suppose I owe you one for all of those delicious cookies you brought into the office."

"Do you have access to the security footage from the bakery?"

"Yes, I do."

"Is there any way that I could take a look at it?" She bit into her bottom lip. "I don't want to get you into any trouble, but it would really help me out."

"It's no trouble. I had to pull some pieces out

from it for the story on the website. Do you want to come by now and have a look?"

"Yes, that would be great! Thank you so much."

"No problem. I know you had nothing to do with this, Brenda, and anything I can do to help you get through this, I'm at your service."

"Thanks Richard." She sighed with relief as she hung up the phone. When she returned to the living room she found Joyce seated on the recliner with Molly in her lap. The rabbit looked up and wiggled her nose as Brenda stepped in.

"I spoke to someone who has access to the tapes. He said we could come take a look right now." She stroked the rabbit's fur.

"Oh wonderful!" Joyce eased Molly off her lap and gathered her purse. "Let's go."

"I'll drive." She grabbed her keys and purse, and they headed out the door.

"So, who is this friend?" Joyce glanced over at her as she started the car.

"Richard. He works for the newspaper, in the video editing department. They have a website where they expand their printed stories with audio and video. He has the tapes because he is putting together something to post on the website to go along with the story." She pulled out of the driveway and drove towards the newspaper office.

"He's not going to try to pump us for a story, is he?" Joyce frowned. "We should be careful what we say."

"No, Richard is a trustworthy guy. Plus, he doesn't write the articles. He just edits the video that will be added to it. And he loves my cookies."

"Your cookies?" Joyce grinned.

"Yes, chocolate chip butterscotch. I'll make him a big batch after all of this is over." She turned down the road that led to the newspaper office.

"I'd love to try some, too. Do you think we're going to run into Charlie?" She looked up at the large three-story building.

"No, it's not likely. He's usually holed up in his office when he's on a deadline. I'd rather not interrupt him. Although, unfortunately I think that this situation is already having an impact on him. He sounded so tired when I spoke to him."

"I'm sorry to hear that." Joyce gazed up at the windows as Brenda parked. "I'm sure he's worried about you, but try not to let it get to you, we're going to get all of this straightened out."

"Hopefully this will be a good start."

As they headed into the building Brenda led the

way to Richard's office. When she knocked on the door, she heard a bit of commotion on the other side. He opened the door as he pulled his headphones off. Tall and wiry, he seemed to just fit into the small room. As he smiled at them, his cheeks flushed.

"Sorry, I had my headphones on and almost fell out of my chair when you knocked. I don't get many visitors."

"Sorry for startling you." Brenda returned his smile. "I guess you didn't expect me to show up so fast."

"No, I didn't. Just give me a few minutes and I'll have it set up for you. I'm going on lunch break anyway, so you can use the room." He leaned over a keyboard that was attached to a large monitor. As he typed, an image appeared on the screen. It was the front of the bakery. A second image popped up beside it, a rear view of the bakery.

"Oh, wow this is great. I didn't know Jerry had so many cameras."

"It is a little unusual for a business on that street to have such good coverage. There's hardly ever any crime there, and most buildings don't have cameras. But I guess Jerry wanted to be thorough. I'm not sure what you're hoping to find, but I've been through all of the footage from that morning, and the only person that goes in or out of the bakery is Jerry." He stepped past them, through the door. "Good luck."

"Great." Joyce sat down in one of the rolling computer chairs. "Should we even bother to look? If no one is on the camera, then we're not going to find out much."

"You may be right." She sighed as she sat down in the chair in front of the keyboard and monitor. "But, what if they're looking in the wrong place?"

"You mean they should be looking somewhere other than the bakery?" Joyce raised an eyebrow.

"No, I should say, maybe they are looking at the wrong time. You heard what Richard said. It is unusual for a business on that street to have so many cameras. So why did he have them? Maybe he experienced something that made him more vigilant. Maybe if we roll back the date and time we'll catch something else unusual on the camera."

"Oh, good idea!" Joyce nodded. "I can also check to see if I can find out when the cameras were purchased and installed." She pulled out her phone. "Is there any information on the company that provided the cameras or where he might have purchased them?"

"Yes, on this note it says Baned Security. But

I'm not sure how much they will tell you." Brenda began to scan through the video footage.

"Hm. Good point. But maybe if I use this phone." Joyce picked up the landline on the desk beside the monitor.

"Good idea." Brenda continued to scroll through the footage. She knew that checking the footage during the day wouldn't reveal much, as Jerry had plenty of customers come and go. Instead she focused on the afterhours portions of the video.

"Yes, I'm calling from Daily News Marsail, and I'd like to find out about a purchase date for some of your equipment." She paused and met Brenda's eyes. "Yes, I have the serial number here." She took the piece of paper that Brenda offered her, then rattled off the number. "Yes, I understand, but we're working on a story and this is part of our verification of information. All I need to know is the date the equipment was purchased, please." She smiled and nodded at Brenda. "Great, thanks so much." She hung up the phone.

"Well? Did they give it to you?" Brenda gazed at her eagerly.

"Yes, he purchased them on October fifth."

"October fifth, why does that sound familiar?"

Brenda narrowed her eyes as she continued to skim through the footage.

"Let me see." Joyce checked the calendar on her phone. "It was the day of the first planning meeting for the holiday market. Jerry was there, remember? He was complaining about not getting a spot at the market."

"Interesting. Do you think he bought them because he thought there would be an uptick of crime due to the market?" She slowed the video down as she spotted something strange on it.

"Maybe. But the market was still months away. It seems a little strange that he would buy them so early. What if something about that meeting made him feel vulnerable? As I recall there wasn't much that stood out about that meeting. They introduced us as new vendors, remember?"

"Yes." She nodded then pointed at the screen. "Look, I think I found something. It looks like someone's shadow on the back door."

"Could it be a trick of light?" Joyce leaned forward to take a closer look.

"I thought so, but when I checked other footage it wasn't there. It's there consistently three days in a row. Like someone is hiding out near the back door." She tapped the screen.

"What is the date on the video?" Joyce studied the screen.

"It's December tenth, eleventh, and twelfth so far. There is still more video to look through."

"Interesting. That's only a few days after the market started and a little over a week ago. I think that it's very possible this person, whoever it is, could have been involved in the murder. If only we had a clear shot of the face, or even the body, we might be able to figure something out."

"There's nothing here. Nothing but a shadow." She sighed as she sat back in her chair. "Another dead-end."

"Not dead necessarily." Joyce pulled out her tablet and logged the dates that Brenda spotted the shadow. "We know that someone was there. We also know that Jerry bought those cameras for a reason, and that was a valid reason, since someone was skulking around the bakery when it was closed. That is somewhere to start, even if we don't have a name or face to go with it."

"That's true." Brenda covered her mouth as a yawn escaped her. "I was just hoping for something more I guess."

"I think we need to rest a bit and let our minds churn through all of this. Let's go back to the house." As she stood up she felt a bite of pain snake its way up along her back. That didn't surprise her, as whenever she was stressed she would get a bit of back pain. Most of the time it would disappear quickly, but once it had landed her in bed for a few days.

"Well, there's nothing more to see here." Brenda turned off the monitor and stood up. As they left the newspaper office, she was tempted to just step in the elevator and head upstairs for a hug from her husband. Instead, she kept her focus on going out the door behind Joyce. Part of starting the donut truck business was about experiencing independence for the first time in a long time. That meant dealing with her own problems, even if Charlie would be more than willing to deal with them for her.

CHAPTER 9

*E*arly the next morning, Brenda woke to the sound of Joyce's phone ringing. It was the second time she'd heard it. The first time she'd ignored it and willed herself to go back to sleep. But the second time she couldn't. She sat up in bed as she heard Joyce's voice through the wall.

"It's very early, Detective."

The moment she heard that, her chest tightened. Why was he calling so early? What news could he have that couldn't wait? She padded out into the hallway, just as Joyce stepped out of her own bedroom.

"I guess he woke you, too, huh?" She shook her head.

"What was it about?" Brenda followed her into the kitchen.

"It was good news, actually, which was surprising. He said he wanted to tell me personally that we've been given the all clear to reopen the truck as of ten this morning." She began to get the coffee pot ready.

"Oh, that is good news!" Brenda smiled. "Does that mean that they've found the killer?"

"No, unfortunately. But the truck has been processed as much as it can be, and the mayor has been putting pressure on the police department to get the market back up and running, so we have the opportunity to open the truck back up."

"Well, that's not great news. But at least we can get back to work."

"He also said that he wants a copy of the gingerbread donut recipe. He wants me to email it to him."

"The gingerbread donuts. Why?" Brenda asked, then her eyes widened. "He thinks they were poisoned?"

"I don't know, but he can think it all he wants. They weren't, so let's just give him the recipe."

"Okay." Brenda nodded slowly.

"Apparently, all of our supplies have been removed as a precaution and the inside of the truck has gone through a special cleaning to sanitize it."

"At least we didn't have a lot of stock delivered.

We are getting most of the dry ingredients delivered this week."

"I know. I can't wait to get back open."

"Do you think anyone will come to the truck, though?" Brenda bit into her bottom lip.

"Why wouldn't they?" Joyce looked into her eyes. "Listen, we didn't do anything wrong."

"I know that. But the last time the detective was here he wouldn't try the donuts I offered him. I mean, people are going to know that Jerry was possibly killed by a donut. Do you really think they're going to risk purchasing anything from us?"

"Yes, I do. Because the regulars will know better, and the visitors won't have a clue about what happened. We'll be fine. Hiding out is not an option. We need to show the detective that we have nothing to hide from. Let him believe what he wants. If he can't solve the crime, well then he's just not very good at his job, is he?" Joyce turned the coffee pot on. "You can decide whether you want to or not, but I'm going to be at the truck by nine. That way we have time to tidy up whatever they might have done to it."

"Yes, I'll be there, of course." Brenda placed a hand on Joyce's shoulder as she turned away from the coffee pot. "I'm sorry, I know I can be a little anxious."

"You have every reason to be. I'm nervous, too. We all show it in different ways. But I'm trying to convince myself that we have nothing to be worried about here." Joyce sighed. "I guess that's a bit of a contradiction."

"This whole thing is a mess. I just wish it was over with." She frowned. "I just keep picturing myself with my arms around Sophie on Christmas Eve. All of this will be behind us by then. Right?"

"Right." Joyce poured them both a cup of coffee. "I say, we go in, we get the truck open, we let everyone see our faces and that we're not worried about anything. It's the only thing we can do right now."

"That's true." Brenda sipped her coffee. "Let me make us some breakfast first, though. We have plenty of time."

"Sounds great to me." She patted her stomach and grinned. "I will never turn down anything you make."

"Thanks Joyce." She was relieved that at least someone would eat her cooking. As she began to prepare breakfast, she wondered what Sophie was waking up to. She guessed it was cinnamon sprinkled hot chocolate. It was one of her mother's specialties. The more time she spent thinking about Sophie, the less tense she felt. Yes, all of this would be over soon. She just had to focus on that. "You know, I never arranged for my tree to be delivered."

"Are you planning to today?" Joyce sniffed the air and smiled at the smell of the french toast that Brenda cooked on the stove.

"They have finished the tiling apparently, it is just drying now. So, I'll have to open up the house and let him deliver it, but yes, I think it would be a good way to take my mind off things. I'll wait until the close of business today, though." She scooped the french toast onto two plates and carried it over to the table. "I'd like to speak to him about his issues with other vendors and whatever else he might know."

"I don't know, he seems like a pretty tough cookie to crack. You should be careful." Joyce rubbed her hands together as she looked at her plate. "This is amazing. I don't know how you make it so fluffy."

"My secret." She winked at her. "I should be okay. He's probably just a little rough around the edges. Although, like you, I do get a strange feeling around him. Then again, I am the nervous type."

She took a bite of her french toast and had to admit that it was delicious.

"You do that too often, you know?" Joyce pointed her fork at her with a bit of french toast on the end.

"What?" She stared at the bobbing bread.

"You second guess yourself, and put yourself down. You have strong instincts, Brenda, that's why you're a bit anxious at times. You sense what's going on in the world around you, more than other people do. It could be your mother's intuition working overtime, but I'd guess that you've always been a lot more perceptive than others."

"Maybe." She smiled some as she took another bite. "I know that I've had moments in my life when I was absolutely certain. Like the day I met Charlie." Her cheeks warmed as she recalled it.

"Sounds like there's a story there?" Joyce raised an eyebrow.

"Honestly, I've never even told him this. I've been afraid that he would find it really strange. But I knew he was the one before he ever really even noticed me. I saw him, I spoke to him, just for a moment, and I knew right then I would spend the rest of my life with him." She shrugged. "It wasn't like a vision or anything. It was just this deep knowing, that we had an entire future together."

"I think that's amazing." Joyce smiled as she met her eyes. "That's exactly what I'm talking about. Your instincts are sharp. So don't pretend that it's just nerves, or paranoia that make you uncomfortable around some people. There's no reason to discredit your strengths."

"You're so good to me, Joyce." She finished her french toast. "I can't tell you how glad I am that we became friends."

"I'm glad, too." She finished her breakfast as well. "Now, we'd better get to work before Detective Crackle changes his mind."

~

On the drive to the truck, Joyce did her best to provide some cheerful chatter, but her attempts soon faded. She was nervous, too, and though Brenda seemed more focused now, Joyce could tell that she was just as frightened. It was hard not to be. Their truck was a crime scene, and despite being able to open it again, the weight of Jerry's death would have quite an impact on everyone at the market.

"Here we go." Brenda parked in one of the vendors' spots, and turned off the car. She looked over at Joyce. "Like you said, we haven't done anything wrong. We have to keep that in mind."

"Yes." She stepped out of the car and tried not to notice the stares from other nearby vendors. It was impossible. "Today will be rough, but once we get through it each day after will get easier and easier."

Brenda nodded as she approached the truck. Both women fell silent as they paused at the steps that led to the door of the truck.

"What a mess." Joyce pushed her hair back from her eyes as she stared at the truck. "You would think they would have cleaned up the egg. I mean, really. Now it's all dried." She sighed as she brushed a finger across the steps. "Disgusting."

"Don't worry, I can have it cleaned up in just a few minutes." Brenda took a deep breath of the crisp air. "Luckily, it's too cold for them to go rotten and start to smell."

"There's that positive attitude." Joyce grinned. "All right I'll let you work out here, and I'll check out the inside. I'm not sure what I expect. I know they said they had cleaned the place, but I'm betting it's still quite a mess." As she started to climb the steps to the door of the truck, she heard a familiar voice not far behind her.

"Joyce, do you have a minute?" Detective Crackle folded his hands behind his back and studied both of the women.

"Sure." Joyce stepped back down and walked over to him, with a glance over her shoulder at Brenda.

"As of now you're free to open and operate. I can't stop the market from happening and we've gathered all of the evidence we can from the truck. However, this investigation is not over. I will get to the bottom of this." His tone and expression softened just slightly as he held Joyce's gaze. "If there is anything you can tell me, anything that you think will help at all. Now would be the time."

"I'm sorry, I don't know anything more than you do, Detective Crackle. All I'm certain of is that Brenda and I had nothing to do with it. You are wasting your time investigating us." She returned his steady stare without a trace of intimidation.

"That may be true." He smiled some behind his mustache. "But I have to follow the path of the investigation. That's my duty."

"Duty." She nodded. "I can understand your dedication to that. My late husband would have been just as dedicated. But don't expect me to be pleased with your intrusion into our lives."

"I suspect that Jerry wasn't pleased with the intrusion into his." He pursed his lips, then relaxed as he studied her. "A man died, whether you liked him or not, that has to be answered for."

"Whether I liked him or not, I want to see his killer brought to justice. What I don't want to see is you focusing on the wrong suspects."

"Suspect." He cleared his throat.

"Excuse me?" Joyce met his eyes.

"How often do you make the donuts on this truck, Joyce?" He looked past her, to Brenda, where she scrubbed at the steps.

"What does that matter?" She took a step closer to him as the urge to protect Brenda welled up within her.

"As I mentioned, we have reason to believe that the poison was in the glaze on a pastry. Possibly a donut. Isn't that what Brenda makes on the truck each day?" He lifted his eyebrows.

"That's ridiculous. Or have you forgotten that Jerry worked in a bakery? He made donuts as well as other pastries, although I'm guessing he wasn't the one that made them." Joyce frowned as she crossed her arms.

"No? Then who did?" He glanced over at Brenda once more, then back to Joyce.

"All I know is that Jerry didn't do much work. I've heard that from his employees. I don't know if it's true or not. I didn't personally know the man very well, nor did I care to." She turned and started to walk back towards the truck. "You can keep focusing on the wrong people, or you can start learning a bit more about the man you considered to be a friend."

"Joyce." He followed after her for a few steps. "I will find out the truth, no matter what it takes."

"We'll see who figures it out first." She glanced over her shoulder at him for a moment, then continued on to Brenda's side. "I'm sorry, that impossible man is driving me up the wall!"

"What did he say?" She lifted her eyes to her friend's, as the sponge in her hand dripped on the truck steps.

"Never mind that, the important thing is that we are going to open up soon and we need to be ready. How is that coming along? Do you want to take a break? I can take over."

"No, it's fine. I've almost got it. Something sticky was under it all, stickier than I would expect an egg to get." She ran the sponge across the steps a few more times. "I know he told you something. Joyce, just tell me what it was."

"They're focusing in on the idea that the poison was disguised in a donut."

"And we, run a donut truck." Brenda smiled some, more out of frustration than amusement, and tossed the sponge back into a bucket. "Things keep looking worse, hmm?"

"I wouldn't say worse. But, well, maybe a little." She frowned as she wondered if she should admit that the detective was focusing in on her. She knew it would frighten Brenda even more than she already was, and though she didn't like to keep things from her, she also didn't want to send her into a panic. "Let's forget about it for now. We have a truck to open up, right?" She smiled.

"Right." Brenda nodded and forced a smile in return.

"I'll go to the store and get the supplies, so we're covered until our order comes in."

"Great, thanks Joyce."

It didn't take long to get the truck into shape, and soon they opened their side window to indicate that they were open. The sweet smell of delicious donuts surrounded them both. Despite the tension that flooded through her, Brenda began to relax.

Whenever she baked, she did. She also hummed. When she first heard the sound come from deep in her throat she wondered if it could really be coming from her. How could she hum at a time like this? But the process of baking had always given her a special sense of calm.

CHAPTER 10

Two hours passed with only two customers who approached the truck. Both were vendors at the market.

"I think they just wanted a look see." Joyce sighed as she gazed out through the open window. "One donut a piece? That's not much of a purchase."

"I'm sorry, Joyce. I knew this would happen." Brenda wiped her hands and turned to look through the window as well. The crowd was more sparse than usual. "I think many people have been scared away by Jerry's death. Maybe tomorrow will be better. Once people have a chance to forget, they'll be back to shop, and eat." She did her best to sound convincing. In reality though, her opinion was less confident. Part of her wondered if a new baker might change the fate of 'Donuts on the Move'. Maybe, if people knew that someone different was baking, they would be less likely to avoid the truck. How could they recover with her on the truck? The thought of never working on the truck again gave her an awful, sinking feeling, but she knew that Joyce had invested a lot in the business, and she didn't want her to lose everything. The more she thought about it, the more emotional she became. She loved working on the truck, baking as a job, helping support Joyce's business, and being part of something with Joyce.

"I'm sure you're right, Brenda. We just need to give it a few days."

"You've always got such a positive outlook, I really appreciate that." Brenda turned towards her with a small smile. She bit into her bottom lip and took a deep breath. She knew that if Joyce caught wind of her feelings, she would be upset.

"It pays to be positive. It really does. But we need more than positive, we need some progress on this case."

"Yes, you're right about that."

"It's painfully slow."

"I have plenty of extra donuts already made so I can serve customers. Why don't you go see if you can track down Aaron? I know he's still out making deliveries. He's usually up to the grocery stores by now, I think." Brenda set another tray of donuts on the counter to cool.

"That's a good idea. I'll see if I can get his schedule from his boss, and if so then maybe he'll be willing to talk. He's our only possible witness to the murder, that we know of." Joyce narrowed her eyes. "And of course he's also a suspect."

"I hate to think that, but yes, until we can clear him he's definitely a suspect."

"Are you sure you don't mind me taking off?" Joyce looked into her eyes. "I know today can't be easy for you."

"It's fine, I promise." She gave her a quick hug. "It'll give me some time to think about how I'm going to approach Gray. Here, take my keys." She handed over the keys to her car.

"All right. If anyone gives you any trouble let me know." Joyce looked into her eyes one more time, then stepped off the truck. It was good to get outside, despite the chill in the air. Being inside of the truck made her think of everything that had and could still go wrong. She felt a bit too confined by it today. As she walked towards the parking lot, she called the company that Aaron worked for. After a few pleas and the promise of free donuts she managed to get his schedule. As usual, Brenda was right, he was at a nearby grocery store delivering a large order of eggs. It only took a few minutes to drive to it. His truck was easy to spot. She parked close to it, and lingered near it as she waited for him to return to it. When she saw him come out of the grocery store pushing an empty metal cart, she stepped out of his line of sight. She didn't want to tip him off that she was there just yet. Instead she studied the way he walked, and his expressions. He pulled the back doors open, and loaded in the cart. He closed the doors on the back of the truck, then turned to walk towards the driver's side door.

"Hello Aaron." She walked up behind him.

He jumped at the sound of her voice, and spun around to face her.

"H-hi." He brushed his hand back through his hair. "Do I know you?"

"My name is Joyce. You deliver eggs to my truck, 'Donuts on the Move'." She smiled. "We haven't really met properly, but we've seen each other, I think."

"Oh." He took a step back, then lowered his eyes. "Yes, I know that truck."

"Yes, that's right, that truck." She studied him

intently as he gazed hard at the ground. "The one where Jerry died. You were there that morning, weren't you, Aaron?"

"I really need to get out and make these deliveries." He started towards the door again.

"I only have a few questions. I'll only be a minute, I promise." She stepped in front of him to stop him.

"I don't have a minute, sorry." He walked past her and reached for the door.

"Aaron." She placed a hand on the curve of the back of his shoulder. "If you have something to say, I'm here to listen."

"What would I have to say?" He peered back over his shoulder at her.

"I can tell that you're upset, Aaron. Did you see something or hear something that scared you?" She searched his eyes when they finally met hers.

"I don't know what you mean." He frowned as he reached for the door again. "I had nothing to do with any of that. Now, I have to go."

"I'm sorry, that's not good enough." She pressed her hand against the door to hold it shut. "You can't pretend that you weren't there that morning, Aaron. You had already delivered the eggs. They were broken all over the steps. Did you drop them?"

"So what, I'd delivered the eggs?" He glared at her as his cheeks reddened. "I don't want any trouble. All right? I just got this job."

"What does that mean exactly?" She searched his expression. "You saw something but you're afraid to come forward about it?"

"I didn't see anything, that's the thing." His brows knitted. "If I had seen something that could help I would have told the police. But I didn't."

"You saw something." Joyce narrowed her eyes and stepped directly in front of him again. "Tell me, Aaron. If you don't want me to report it to the detective, I won't. But my good friend and I are in a lot of trouble over this. We didn't do anything to harm Jerry. You know we didn't, don't you?"

"Yes, I know." He looked up at her so swiftly that it surprised her. "I know your cars weren't in the parking lot. I know that Jerry was inside of your truck, and he was alone."

"How do you know that? What exactly did you see?"

"Look, in order to make all of the deliveries on time, I get to the building an hour early. I don't clock in, I just load up the truck, make a couple of deliveries and then go back to the building and clock in. I don't want to lose this job, and I knew if I couldn't make the runs on time, if they find out that I was using the truck without being clocked-in, I'm going to be fired on the spot."

"Okay, don't worry, I won't tell anyone. But you need to tell me exactly what you saw. Understand?"

"It's not enough. It's not going to matter." He ran his hand back through his short hair.

"Just tell me, Aaron. Please." She placed her hand on his shoulder, and the young man gazed at her with the fragility of a lost child. "I know that it probably scared you, that it still scares you, but it's so very important."

"I was delivering the eggs on the steps, when I saw some movement inside the truck." His jaw tensed and he looked away from her.

"It's okay, Aaron, just tell me." She gave his shoulder a reassuring pat.

"I looked inside, because I thought it was odd, and I saw him through the window. I think he saw me, too. He had this weird look on his face. I was scared. I dropped the eggs and started to run, but when I turned, there was a figure right there beside the steps. I couldn't see him, it was dark, but he was there. I thought they were teamed up to rob the truck or something. Real heroic, right?" His cheeks were bright pink as he stared down at his feet. "I just took off. When I calmed down, I thought about calling the police, but when I rolled back through the police were already there. I didn't know he was dead until later. I swear."

"Aaron, you say that Jerry was alive when you saw him?"

"He was." He swallowed hard. "His eyes were wide, I thought because he saw me. But, now, I don't know. Maybe he was scared. I should have done something to stop all of this. I should have confronted the guy in the shadows."

"You have no idea who he was?"

"No, I'm sorry. I didn't see his face. It was more like I sensed him there, and when I caught a glimpse of him, I took off. I thought he was going to come after me." His cheeks grew hot again. "I'm sorry. I should have done something."

"There was nothing you could have done." She asked a few more questions and made a few notes, then patted his shoulder as she looked back at him. "You've helped a lot, Aaron. Just one more thing. Did the eggs crack when you dropped them?"

"Maybe a bit, but I don't think so. I just dropped the crates on the steps."

"You didn't step on them? You're sure?"

"I'm sure." He frowned. "Are you going to tell the detective?"

"Not if I don't have to." She studied him a moment longer. As she walked away from the truck she couldn't help but wonder if he was telling the truth. Maybe he'd made up the whole story to try to hide the fact that he'd been the one to kill Jerry. One glance back at his pink cheeks, made her doubt that he would be capable of hurting an insect, much less a human being.

~

Brenda decided against making another batch of donuts. She already doubted that all of the donuts she'd made so far would be sold. As she watched people pass by the truck she continued to feel down about the possibility that her presence was going to ruin the chances of their business succeeding.

A few minutes later, Detective Crackle's face appeared in the window of the truck.

"Brenda." He smiled. "Do you have a minute to chat?"

Her heart thumped against her chest. She didn't want to face him alone.

"I was just going to start a new batch of donuts." She turned away from the window.

"It sure looks like you have plenty already made." He cleared his throat. "I notice you have quite a few of those gingerbread donuts."

"Yes, they're pretty popular. Well, they are usually." She avoided looking directly at him. Then she worried that might make her look more guilty.

"What I find interesting, is the white, red and green glaze." He gestured to the tray. "May I see one up close?"

Her heart continued to pound. The last thing she wanted was to get any closer to him. However, she also didn't want him to have a bad impression of her. She grabbed a donut with a paper napkin and set it on a plate.

"Free of charge." She managed to smile.

"Oh no, thanks, I don't want to eat it." He eyed the donut, then snapped a picture of it with his phone. "You see, the medical examiner gave me a list of Jerry's stomach contents. Not much was digested. But the limited contents matches the recipe Joyce sent me. The substance on his lips was confirmed as glaze and it was an unusual color combination. Much like the glaze on this donut. In fact, I would say, that this particular type of donut is exactly what he ate that morning. But, I'm guessing, this donut isn't laced with poison, is it?"

"Of course not." Shocked, she made the mistake of looking into his eyes. "I'm sure it wasn't one of our donuts that he ate."

"Are you?" He stared hard into her eyes. "Because your truck is the only one selling this particular donut in the area, and this particular color combination of glaze. Red, white and green. The exact combination that was found on Jerry's lips. But, it wasn't your donut?"

"No!" She blinked back tears. "No, it certainly wasn't. Unless." She swallowed hard. "Unless, someone bought a donut and poisoned it."

"Now that's a stretch, isn't it? Why would anyone buy one of your donuts just to poison it? I mean, that would be a silly thing to do. They could have poisoned anything. Why your donut?"

"I don't know." She clenched her hands into fists at her sides. "But if it was one of our donuts, then that must have been what happened."

"Sure." He snapped another picture of the donut. "Thanks for your time."

As he walked away, she snatched up the donut. Her entire body grew hot as a mixture of anger and panic rushed over her.

When her cell phone rang she was relieved to have a distraction. The sight of Charlie's name on the screen even brought about a smile.

"Hi there, sweetie." She leaned back against the rear counter and closed her eyes as she savored the sound of his voice.

"Hey. Why didn't you come up and see me when you were here yesterday?"

"I knew you were busy." She frowned. "I didn't want to bother you."

"I'm always here for you, no matter what. I would have loved to see you."

"Please, don't be upset with me, Charlie. I just didn't want to bother you." She sighed. "I'm pretty sure everyone around here thinks I poisoned Jerry."

"Oh hon, they don't think that. People just love a juicy rumor. I'm not upset with you. I just wish you had come to see me. I miss you."

"I miss you, too. Maybe teaming up with Joyce and running this truck was a mistake, Charlie."

"Do you really think that?" Joyce's voice drifted to her from the entrance of the truck.

Brenda gulped as she saw the hurt in her friend's expression. "Charlie, I have to go. I'll call you later." She hung up the phone.

"Brenda." Her face grew pale. "You're not serious, are you?"

"It's all my fault, Joyce. It was my donut that he ate, that was poisoned. No one is ever going to believe that I had nothing to do with this. I'm going to end up in jail, and even if I don't, our reputation will be ruined. I think you'd be better off if you started looking for a new baker."

"Absolutely not." Joyce stepped up to her with a look of determination in her eyes. "Let me tell you something, young lady, I have never in my life known a more talented baker, or a better friend. None of this is your fault. How could it possibly be? I'm not going to give up. Are you?"

"No." Brenda sighed and wiped at her eyes. "I don't want to. But I just don't know what to do. Detective Crackle was here, you should have seen the way he looked at me. Joyce, I'm ready to run to Mexico with Charlie and Sophie, that's how scared I am."

"Oh hon." She gave her a tight hug. "You're not going anywhere. Don't worry about that detective. He is just doing his job. Just take a few deep breaths, all right? I found out some interesting information from Aaron and I think it's going to help us."

"Okay." She took a few deep breaths, and the panic within her began to settle. Joyce always knew how to help her calm down. "What did you find out?"

Joyce recounted the conversation she'd had with Aaron. "This pretty much proves that we were not at the truck when Jerry died."

"But that doesn't matter, does it? Because the donut could have been poisoned at any time."

"That's true, and now that we know what kind of donut it was, we might be able to figure out who bought it. But more importantly, we know that someone else was there. Aaron saw a figure by the truck, and he put the eggs down, and ran."

"But a figure doesn't solve anything." Brenda grimaced as she tried to hold back a frustrated groan.

"No, but that figure had feet. Because when we arrived, the eggs were trampled. So that means someone climbed up those steps and peered inside to make sure that Jerry was dead. Why else would anyone stomp all over the eggs and then not call the police when they saw Jerry?"

"Yes, okay." Brenda's heart started to calm. "So, we know that someone was there between the time that Aaron delivered the eggs, and we arrived, which was only a small span of time."

"Correct. And, whoever poisoned the donut, used one of ours. Can you remember anyone buying a donut that stood out to you?"

"Oh Joyce, those were the most popular donuts we sold. But wait." Her eyes widened. "Yes, the employees from Jerry's store. We gave them some, remember?"

"Aha." Joyce smiled. "See, we're getting closer and closer to the truth. I think it's time for me to pay a visit to the bakery."

CHAPTER 11

When Joyce arrived at the bakery she found the door locked and a closed sign in the window. But, she could see lights on, and Orville inside. She knocked on the door until he finally came and opened it.

"What is it?"

"Can I come in and speak to you for a few minutes, please?" She offered her most charming smile.

"Sure." He shrugged. "Careful, the floor is wet. I'm trying to get this place cleaned up."

He locked the door behind her.

"I'll only be a minute. I'm surprised to see you here. I thought Jerry fired you?"

"He did. But he also left me the bakery in his

will. So here I am. What do you want to talk about?" He looked up at her as he picked up a mop. Joyce listened closely and tried not to react. Orville was fired then inherited the bakery, that certainly gave him motive, didn't it?

"I know that you were very upset about Jerry firing you." Joyce watched as he slid the mop across the floor.

"I was." He glanced up at her. "Why wouldn't I be? That doesn't make me a murderer."

"No, it doesn't. Please don't think that's my belief. I just wonder, was there something else going on between you two that made things so tense?"

"No." He swept the mop across the floor again. "The thing is, Jerry wasn't such a terrible guy. Most people will tell you he was. I know he gave you a hard time." He glanced up at her again. "But when you really got to know him, which took a very long time, he had a pretty decent soul underneath. He donated a portion of his profits to charity, and he always made sure those that couldn't afford it had a pie during the holidays. He was a jerk, for sure. He didn't like people on the whole, I'm guessing not even himself. But he wasn't such a bad guy, deep down. He had a soft spot for those less privileged."

"That's kind of you to say considering that he

treated you so badly." She crossed her arms and kept her gaze on him. "It's so easy to overlook the good in people."

"I don't know what happened to Jerry. But I do know, he didn't deserve it. Nobody does." He set the mop back in the bucket and looked across the wet floor at her. "So why are you really here, Joyce? Because I doubt it's to chat about Jerry."

"Honestly?"

"Yes. I'd like to know."

"I thought you might know why he was on the donut truck. I can't seem to get over the fact that he was there. He had no reason to be. I'm certain that he stole a key from my purse, and that was how he got in. But why? What were his intentions?"

"What do you think?" He sneered as he shook his head. "He hated that you guys were there instead of him and that Brenda had those festive gingerbread donuts. He wanted to know how to make them, but he couldn't find a recipe that matched it. So, he sent Mark and Clarence to buy some from the truck. That's what Mark told me, anyway."

"Are you talking about me?" Mark popped his head out through the kitchen doors.

She noticed that he had a mop as well.

"Never mind, Mark, just finish cleaning up back there."

"I've been cleaning for ages. I finally got all the caramel from the cupcakes off the floor."

"Good." Orville nodded. "That stuff is so sticky. It was all over my shoes. We need to have this place cleaned up by tomorrow."

"What's tomorrow?" Her eyes locked on Orville.

"We have Jerry's estate lawyers coming in, to look at the place." Orville met her eyes. "It's not like we can just open for business."

"Right, I understand." Joyce did her best to ignore the dig. Did he think they had reopened too soon. "What about the donuts?" She looked back at Mark. "What did you do with them?"

"Like Orville said, Jerry had us buy some so he could try one and see if he could figure out the recipe. They were the ones Brenda landed up giving us for free, remember?"

"Yes. Did Jerry try one?" She held her breath.

"I left them on the counter for him, he'd already gone home for the night. I guess he ate one in the morning when he came in?" He shrugged. "There was one missing from the box. I gave the rest to the police."

"You did?" Her heart skipped a beat. Maybe that was what had the detective so confident. Had they found poison in the other donuts as well?

"Yes, the detective asked for them."

"Who else was here with you when you left that night?" She held his gaze.

"No one. Everyone else had already gone home." He glanced towards Orville.

She noticed the way he kept looking at Orville, as if maybe he was checking for approval of his statements. Whether or not he was, he seemed very nervous.

"Did you ever notice Jerry having any conversations with any other people? Any other issues?"

"Only everyone." Orville chuckled. "But you know that already."

"I mean anyone specific. Did you ever see anyone hanging around the bakery, maybe while you were closing up?" She looked between the two men.

"Yes, actually." Mark stepped towards her. "The guy, from the tree stand. He would be standing outside every morning when I opened. I'd ask him if he wanted a muffin or anything, and he'd say no. I thought it was weird, because why stand there if he didn't want anything?" He shrugged. "But then one morning he wasn't there anymore. So, I just forgot about it."

"Gray? I wonder what he was doing."

"Smoking." Orville narrowed his eyes. "I've seen him smoke a few times near the bakery. There's an ashtray there. I figured he didn't want to smoke near the trees, it could be a fire hazard."

"True." She smiled. "Thanks for your time." She looked between the two again. "Good luck with the cleaning."

"Thanks." Orville watched her as she walked back out of the bakery. Once outside, she looked in the direction of the tree stand. It was barely visible from where she stood. She was sure there were places that Gray could have smoked closer to his stand. So why did he come all the way over to the bakery just to smoke?

~

*B*renda finished packing away the last of the donuts as Joyce walked up the steps and into the truck.

"How did it go?" Brenda wiped down the counter.

"Interesting." Joyce shared the information she'd been given, focusing specifically on Gray's lingering around the bakery.

"Well, I'm about to go speak with him. Maybe he can give me an explanation for that." She tossed the rag into the sink. "It's almost closing time, so we can start shutting everything down. Is that okay with you?"

"Yes, of course. Are you sure you want to talk to Gray alone?"

"Yes, I think it might be best if I did. We've already talked before, so he might be more relaxed if it's just me."

"Good thinking." Joyce gave her a quick hug. "I'll finish up here, and we'll meet up in the parking lot, all right?"

"Sounds good." Brenda smiled at her before she headed down the steps. As much as she wanted to be positive for Joyce, she was struggling to be positive for herself. But maybe Gray was up to something. And Joyce had mentioned that Mark was looking to Orville for approval of everything he said. Why was that? Maybe they had teamed up together to cause Jerry's death. After all, he had fired Orville, and without Orville, the bakery was destined to fail.

When Brenda arrived at the tree stand, she noticed that Gray stood over near a bundle of wire and wooden pallets. He picked up a watering can and strolled towards the trees. She ducked back as he walked past. She could see him out of the corner of her eye. She didn't want him to know that she was watching. If he looked in her direction, she wasn't sure how she would react. Luckily his focus remained on the trees that he watered. He filled each pot up as he walked by. She noticed the methodical way he moved. He didn't just slosh the water out, he knew precisely how much to put in, and jerked the bucket up in exactly the same way each time. Despite taking the time to be so precise, he also moved very quickly. As he disappeared into the jungle of trees she wondered just what he might know about the murder. She'd volunteered to speak to him, but now she was second guessing herself.

Gray didn't seem like the type to enjoy conversation, especially not a conversation about murder. But without more information she and Joyce would have nothing to go on. It seemed to her that Joyce was much better at talking to people than she was. Still, she put one foot in front of the other and approached him. When she neared the middle of the trees, she recalled overhearing Jerry's angry voice through the branches, not that long before. A voice that would never be heard again.

"We're closed!"

The sudden gruff voice made her jump in fear. Somehow Gray had gotten behind her.

"Oh sorry, I just…" She cleared her throat. "You had said you would deliver the tree sometime, and I thought maybe we could make plans to do that."

"Eh?" He narrowed his eyes as he studied her. "Oh, that's right, I remember you now. All right, you got your ticket?"

"Yes, I do." She fumbled in her purse for it.

"Looks good." He nodded. "Can't tonight, though. It's going to have to be tomorrow, I'll have to arrange a specific time tomorrow. Is that a problem?"

"No, it's fine." She swallowed hard as his steely eyes bored into hers.

"What are you so nervous about?" He took a step towards her.

"Sorry, it's just, this thing with Jerry dying, I'm just a little jumpy."

"I bet." He chuckled. "I hear he ate a poisoned donut. Was it one of yours, girly?" He smirked.

"I heard you liked to hang out near his bakery." She locked her eyes to his, suddenly bold and determined. Perhaps it was him calling her 'girly' or the look of amusement in his eyes over her fear. Whatever it was, she wasn't letting him off the hook.

"Oh, did you?" He scratched his hair-covered cheek. "Well, that might be the case. I can hang out wherever I want, can't I?" He reached into his pocket and pulled out a pack of cigarettes. She watched as he lit a cigarette, right beside the trees. No, he wasn't worried about smoking near his trees. So what had he been doing over by the bakery?

"Sure. But it makes me wonder why. You're not from around here, are you? I mean, you've only lived in the area a short time. You took over the farm from someone else, didn't you?"

"You want to know my life story?" He bit down on the cigarette and made it dance between his lips. "I ain't got one. All right? I don't have any family left. I'm alone and I intend to stay that way. Now, like I said, I'm closed."

He turned and plodded back through the trees. She watched him go, tempted to ask him more questions. But she doubted he would answer them. The important thing was, she knew he was obviously new in town, and that he hadn't been standing next to the bakery just to use the ashtray. He was definitely up to something.

On the drive home with Joyce, Brenda was still a little wound up from her encounter with Gray. She shared what she'd discovered. After they arrived at Joyce's house they had a light dinner, mostly in silence. Finally, Joyce put her fork down and looked across the table at her.

"Tell me again about your plans for Christmas?"

"I already have." She frowned.

"I'd like to hear them again." Joyce smiled.

"How can I even think about enjoying the holiday when I am faced with the possibility of being arrested for murder?" She sighed as she looked at Joyce. "I'm sorry, I know you're just trying to cheer me up. But I just don't feel very cheerful. I don't think we're getting anywhere with what we've found out so far. If we don't figure out who the killer is soon, this may hang over our heads for the rest of our lives."

"I can't disagree with that, Brenda, but giving in to our fear isn't going to .solve things, either. We know that Aaron saw the shadow of a man near the truck that morning. Maybe the figure caught Jerry in the act of entering our truck, and confronted him, only to have him die moments later." Joyce narrowed her eyes. "That doesn't make him the killer, but it does mean that Jerry was alive at that time. We have an idea of when he died."

"Yes, but that still doesn't tell us who it was. I mean, Orville could have poisoned the donuts the night before, or Clarence, or Mark. Or anyone who had access to the bakery." She stroked the rabbit's ears. "I just don't know how we can pin down who it was."

"Aaron said he didn't see our cars in the parking lot, but I wonder if he can recall what cars he did see? Maybe we should check with him about that."

"That's a good idea." Brenda stifled a yawn. "I think I'm ready for bed. I'm exhausted, and tomorrow we need to be up early to open the truck. After I've done the baking I have a few errands to run. Will you be okay to run the truck for a little while?"

"Of course. Having a little break will be good for you. I want to get to the truck very early so I can talk to Aaron again, and see who arrives around the time that Jerry died. Then you can come in normal time."

"Are you sure?" She frowned. "I can come in with you."

"No, there's no need." She patted her hand. "Get some rest. Okay?"

"I'll try."

CHAPTER 12

The next morning Brenda rushed around running her errands. As Joyce had indicated, it was a good distraction. At least it was, until she realized something that startled her. She could see a car in her rearview mirror. It was still there. Just like it had been when she left the bank. Just like it had been when she rolled by the house to check on things. With Charlie so busy at work he didn't have time to pick up the mail or collect the trashcans. She'd parked in front of the house, and noticed the car parked on the other side of the road a few houses down. But no one got out. She was being followed. If her suspicions were right, it was the detective. But she couldn't see the car closely enough to tell.

Brenda had thought that she'd seen a glimpse of

him as she pulled out of the bank. Then she told herself that she was being paranoid. After she finished at the house, she decided to test her theory. After a few turns, she saw the car was still behind her. She headed back the opposite way. So did the car behind her. She turned down a dirt road that was hardly ever used. So did the car behind her. When she came out onto the main road, she got pinned at a red light. The car behind her slowed and turned into a driveway instead of stopping behind her. Once more she wondered if she was just being paranoid. A local wouldn't hesitate to use the dirt road. After the light turned green, she headed back in the direction of Joyce's house. That was when she noticed the car again, not far behind her.

"This is insane!" She gunned the gas, something she rarely ever did, and passed the car in front of her. With some space between herself and the other car, she began to relax. Then the car behind her turned off the road, and there was that same car again.

She gritted her teeth and did her best to keep panic from seizing her senses. Why would the detective be following her? Was he just waiting for the right opportunity to arrest her? Was he collecting evidence against her? She began to go over in her mind all of the errands she'd run in the past few hours. Had he witnessed all of them? Had she done anything that would be considered unlawful? She was sure she'd failed to signal a few times, and there was that one stop sign that she always rolled through because it was in the middle of nowhere. But he hadn't pulled her over.

"Because he's a detective, Brenda!" She shouted at herself. "He's not interested in traffic violations, he wants to arrest you for murder."

When Brenda pulled up at Joyce's she looked down the street, but she couldn't spot him.

She let herself into Joyce's house. In a panic, she texted Joyce to ask her to come home. Within the hour, her car pulled into the driveway. When she stepped inside, Brenda greeted her at the door.

"Oh, Joyce. I'm so glad you're here," Brenda said frantically.

"What's wrong, Brenda? Are you okay?" Joyce looked into her wide eyes.

"It's that detective, I know it is. He was following me around all day today. Everywhere I went, he was there. It's happening, Joyce, he's going to take me in." She shivered as she continued to speak. "The donuts were poisoned, I'm the one that made the donuts, of course he's going to arrest me!"

"Just try to take a deep breath." She ran her hands up and down her arms. "No one is going to take you anywhere."

"Okay, I'm trying to be calm." Brenda chewed on her bottom lip.

"I spoke to Aaron this morning, he was late with his delivery, but turned up shortly after you left. He said that he noticed a few cars in the parking lot, he couldn't tell me who they all belonged to, but he said one was someone's that worked at the bakery, he didn't know his name, and one of them was Gray's truck," Joyce explained as she took off her jacket and boots and left them by the front door.

"Interesting." Brenda's eyes widened. "So, he was there when Jerry died?"

"It sure seems that way."

A knock on the front door made them both jump.

Brenda stared in its direction with wide eyes.

"It's him, Joyce, it's the detective. He's come to arrest me, I know it."

"No, he hasn't." She put her hands on her shoulders and looked into her eyes. "He can't arrest you. You haven't done anything wrong. There's no reason to be scared."

"I have a six-year-old, Joyce, I can't go to

prison. Please, just don't answer the door." Brenda's heart pounded as she visualized the handcuffs on her wrists. How would she ever explain that to Charlie, or Sophie? There would be no way to turn back time the moment that Joyce let him in.

"It will make things worse if we don't answer. The car is in the driveway, he knows that we're here. I have to answer." She sighed and patted her friend's cheek with a light reassuring touch. "Go into my room. In the closet in there. Stay there until I come to get you."

"What if he comes looking?" Her eyes widened as there was another set of knocks on the door.

"He's not going to. I promise. Now just go get tucked away, if that makes you feel more secure. I can guarantee you, Brenda, Detective Crackle will not even know you're here. Trust me." She looked straight into her eyes. "I can handle this."

"Okay." She gulped down a breath of air, then turned and headed for Joyce's room. On the way there she grabbed an umbrella from the hallway. She wasn't sure what she intended to do with it, but she felt better just having something to hold on to. Once she'd ducked into the closet, she heard a third set of knocks, far more insistent this time. Then she heard the sound of the front door as it swung open.

"Detective." Joyce's voice carried through the house. "You'll have to forgive me, I was occupied with some personal needs."

"Personal needs?" He stared at her through squinted eyes. "What exactly does that mean?"

"If I told you exactly what it meant, we'd both be blushing, Detective. How can I help you?" She gritted her teeth as she did her best to hide any hint of fear. Seeing Brenda's concern had left her a little anxious as well.

"Oh, I see, excuse me." He cleared his throat. "Actually, I'm here to speak with Brenda. She's still staying with you, isn't she?"

"Yes, she is." She forced a smile to her lips. "But she's not here right now."

"Her car is in the driveway." He glanced over his shoulder, then looked back at her.

"A friend picked her up." She folded her arms across her stomach and studied him.

"What friend?" He pulled out his notepad.

"I'm not sure that's really my place to say. Why are you looking for her?" She met his eyes.

"I have some more questions I'd like to ask her about the donuts she made on the truck." He tapped his pen against the notepad. "This would be a lot easier if she would just make herself available to me for questioning."

"I don't think she is doing anything other than having a little time out with a friend. That doesn't mean she's avoiding you." She shrugged. "I'll give her the message as soon as I see her."

"Or I could just call her." He pulled out his phone.

Her heart dropped. Brenda's phone was on the kitchen table. Unless she had taken it with her to the closet, it was still there, and not very far from the front door.

"You could, but she's finally getting a little free time with a friend. Is it really necessary to disrupt that?" She took a step forward, which forced him to take a step back out of the doorway. "It's such a beautiful day today, isn't it?" She stepped forward again, under the guise of looking up at the sky. As she pulled the door closed behind her, she heard the first subtle chirp of Brenda's phone ringing inside. But did he?

The detective quirked his brow as he held the phone to his ear. More chirps sounded inside the house.

"I've just been so looking forward to the snow coming. I know it's freezing, but I find the cool air refreshing." She tried not to shiver as she rambled on. She'd stepped outside with no jacket, and just socks on her feet. The icy air bit into her bones. "Do you like snow, Detective?" She could only hope that her voice was enough to drown out the sound of the phone ringing.

"Are you sure she's not in there?" He hung up the phone and stared hard at her. "You wouldn't be obstructing an investigation, would you?"

"I would never." She patted the curve of his elbow. "Go on, I'm sure you have important work to do, and as soon as I hear from her, I'll let you know." She winked at him.

"This isn't over, Joyce, not by a long shot." He continued to hold her gaze, despite the wink and the sweetness in her voice. "You're not fooling me. I know you're trying to cover for her."

"You're wrong." The sweetness disappeared from her voice and her eyes narrowed sharply as she looked at him. "There's nothing to cover for. She's done nothing wrong."

"Hm. So you say." He pulled his hat down low over his forehead and gazed at her from beneath the brim of it. "I'm going to find out the truth one way or another, Joyce. It might be best if you tell me now."

"There's nothing to tell, Detective, other than the fact that I'm going to file charges for harassment if you continue to come after my friend as if she is some kind of murderer. She is a mother."

"I'll investigate all suspects equally." He frowned as he studied her. "I can't bend the rules. I'm sure you can understand that."

"I cannot. I can see this all clearly, while you seem to have tunnel vision. Consider how it is going to feel when you recognize how much of your time you wasted on a wild goose chase." She tried to sound fierce, but her teeth had begun to chatter.

"That's why you are out here freezing in the cold?" He reached out, and to her surprise, grazed his warm fingertips along her hand. "You're like ice. Go back inside."

"I'm fine." She tightened her arms and tried to hide the trembling in her body.

"Don't worry, I'm not going to force my way in." He held her gaze for a long moment. "But keep in mind that I don't like my investigation being hindered in any way."

"Yes sir. I would never dream of doing anything like that." She crept back towards the door.

"I suppose that Brenda will give me a call back, when she sees I called." He held up his cell phone as if he might call her one more time. Instead, he turned and walked back towards his car, which was parked on the street.

Despite the chill that carried through Joyce's bones she waited until he was in his car, with the engine running, before she opened the door to the house. As she suspected, Brenda's phone was ringing. He had planned to listen when she opened the door to go inside. Annoyed, she marched down the hall to her bedroom.

"It's okay, Brenda, you can come out now. He's gone."

"Are you sure?" She poked her head out through the closet door.

"I am. I watched, to make sure he was gone." She grabbed a blanket from the end of her bed and wrapped it around herself. "It was so cold out there!"

"I'm so sorry, Joyce. I hate to put you in the middle of this, but I was just so scared." She frowned as she stepped all the way out of the closet. "I heard my phone ringing."

"Yes, that detective was trying to figure out where you were. He is really sneaky." Joyce narrowed her eyes. "We're going to have to stay on top of this, Brenda. I think he has something, more than we think."

"But he can't have anything. I didn't do anything." She rubbed her upper arms to try to help her warm up. "What could it be?"

"I don't know, but until we find out, you should lay low. Do your best to stay out of his way." Joyce shrugged the blanket off. "I'm warmer now."

"Good." Brenda sighed and looked towards the bedroom door. "I should let Charlie know what's going on. He's going to be upset, but he might be able to help. I just hate to bother him when he's on a deadline."

"I think it's time to stop worrying about that deadline. We need all of the help we can get."

"I guess you're right." She picked up her phone and dialed his number as she walked out into the living room. Joyce followed after her and settled on the couch. After two rings, Charlie answered.

"I was just going to call you."

"You were?" She smiled, glad to hear his voice.

"Yes. I found out something interesting. Jerry was going by an alias. His true identity hasn't been discovered, yet. But the identity he was using was from someone that has been deceased for years."

"Jerry? I never would have believed that about

him." She frowned. "What makes someone assume a new identity?"

"It could be a lot of things, but none of them are good."

"How did you find this out? You've been looking into him?"

"Sure. Honey, you're not alone in this. There seems to be a lot more going on behind the scenes about this. He has such a seamless new identity that it took a lot of digging to figure it out. He either knew how to hide, or had someone help him that knew how to make someone disappear."

"Interesting."

"What is it?" Joyce scooted forward on the couch, her eyes eager.

After Brenda hung up the phone she filled Joyce in on what Charlie shared with her.

"So, he was on the run. Or hiding from someone."

"Someone who might have wanted to kill him." Joyce snapped her fingers.

"The problem is, no one seems to know anything personal about Jerry. I think you should talk to Detective Crackle about Jerry." Brenda sat down across from her on the couch.

"Why would you suggest that? I don't see how

speaking to the detective investigating us could benefit us."

"Everyone I've spoken to about Jerry, knew nothing real about him. According to what Charlie found, he was living under an assumed identity. But didn't you tell me that Detective Crackle was friends with Jerry?"

"Yes, he did tell me that. He acted as if he knew him pretty well, actually and said nice things about him. They seemed very close." Joyce narrowed her eyes.

"So maybe he knows something that we don't."

"Hm. That is a good point." Joyce met her eyes. "Besides the fact that he seems to have something on us and is coming after us at the moment, I actually consider him a pretty good detective. So how could it be that Jerry didn't con anyone else, but him into being his friend?"

"And how is it that a good detective, an experienced one like Detective Crackle, didn't figure out that Jerry was living under a secret identity?" She pursed her lips.

"Are you implying that maybe Detective Crackle knew that Jerry had a secret identity?"

"I'm implying that either he is a very bad detective, or he knows a lot more about Jerry than he is saying. Which is why I think you should talk to him."

"Okay, I think I will. But what makes you think he'll talk to me?" Joyce shook her head. "I wasn't exactly friendly to him just now."

"I've seen the way that he looks at you. Whether you believe me or not, he will talk to you." Brenda stood up from the couch and began to pace. When she glanced back at Joyce, she noticed the woman's hard stare. "I'm serious, Joyce. He respects you, at the very least. He's certainly not going to talk to me."

"Maybe you're right. I'll give it a try. I'll see if I can schedule an appointment with him." She pulled out her phone. Her thoughts were on Detective Crackle, and what his investigation might lead to. If Brenda was right, and he did know more about Jerry than he was revealing, what did that mean? Was he protecting Jerry from something? Was he a crooked cop and covering up for someone's crime? It made her feel terrible to think that and she didn't really believe it. In all the years that she was a cop's wife, there was one thing that her husband hated above all else, and that was a crooked cop. He said they made it hard for people to know who to trust, and did more damage to the criminal justice system than any criminal ever could. That opinion had stuck with her over the years, and now the thought of being face to face with one made her even more uncomfortable. When she heard his voice, her muscles tensed.

"Hello Detective, this is Joyce."

"I know it's you, Joyce. How can I help you?"

"Can I make an appointment to see you sometime today, please?"

"Sure, would you like me to come out to the house?"

She tried to detect his reaction to the request in his voice, but his tone was indifferent.

"No, actually. Would you be available to meet me for lunch?"

"Excuse me?"

She grimaced. Had she pushed too far? The idea of having him out of his element was very appealing to her. But what if he thought her invitation was a little too suspicious?

"I just thought it might be nice for us to have lunch and a conversation. We need to clear the air, and I'm sure that you haven't been eating well while working this case." She put as much sweetness as she could summon into her voice.

"How could you know that?" He chuckled. "I've been on a diet of coffee and junk food."

"I remember when my husband would get involved in a case. He wouldn't eat anything proper for days. I would just show up wherever he was with some home cooked meals. They were prepared by him and then frozen, I have to admit, but it's the thought that counts. Even though he took some ribbing from his partner, he would quiet down when he saw there was enough for two."

"Ah, I see. Yes, a good meal sounds like a great idea. So we'll meet at about one?"

"Yes. There's a little café not far from here. Blue's Place, do you know it?"

"Yes, I've been there a few times. I'll see you soon."

After he hung up the phone, she stared at it for a moment.

"Did he bite?" Brenda looked into her eyes.

"I hope he doesn't." Joyce winced.

CHAPTER 13

*J*oyce parked outside the café and scanned the other cars in the parking lot. Was he already there? She looked for his beat-up old car. As she scanned the parking lot she grew nervous. What would she say when she went inside? How would he react to the questions she would ask? How would she phrase the questions? She spotted his car as she gripped the steering wheel and realized that she wouldn't have much time to decide as she spotted him. He stood near the front door of the café in his suit with his hat pulled down low on his head.

For a split-second she considered pulling back out of the parking space. Although she agreed with Brenda's suspicions, she wasn't sure that she wanted to draw any more of Detective Crackle's attention to herself. She could just cut her losses and head home. But that wouldn't get the crime any closer to being solved. If she really wanted to see justice served then she would have to put in the effort, even if that meant taking a big risk.

As she approached the door, the detective offered her a small smile.

"You took an awful long time to get out of the car."

"You spotted me, huh?" She paused at the bottom of the steps.

"Only after you spotted me." He pulled his hat off and reached for the door of the café. "So you decided to stay?"

"Yes." She smiled as she stepped through the door. When they reached an empty table, he sat down across from her.

"Why are we here, Joyce?"

"Can't we order first?" She raised an eyebrow and picked up the menu.

"I suppose." He picked up his menu and perused it as well. "But putting off the reason for this meeting isn't going to make it any easier to explain after the food arrives."

"I asked you to lunch, you accepted." She peeked over the top of the menu at him.

"That doesn't explain why we are here." He set his menu down.

"What can I get you two?" The waitress smiled at them both as she tapped her pencil against a notepad. "Something sweet?"

"I'll just have the soup of the day." Joyce handed the waitress her menu.

"The same." He handed over his menu as well.

"He'll have a sandwich as well. Turkey, I think. Turkey, Detective Crackle?" She looked across the table at him.

"Yes, fine." He frowned as he studied her. "I am more hungry than I thought. I can't say that I've had anyone order my lunch for me, ever."

"It's important that you keep up your strength."

"I suppose it is." He cleared his throat.

Once the waitress walked away, Joyce felt the pressure of his gaze on her. He wasn't going to let her slide. She had to give him some kind of explanation. The only problem was, she wasn't sure what.

"I've been looking into Jerry's life a bit."

"Oh?" He pushed his hat closer to the edge of the table in anticipation of the food being delivered. "Why would you do something like that?"

"Well, for one, he died on my truck and I'd like to know more about him. And for two, I want to

177

make sure that whoever did this to him is punished for it." She watched him intently as he nodded.

"And, what did you find?"

"Not much so far. It seems that Jerry was a real mystery." She folded her hands, one on top of the other, and studied him. "At least to most people around here."

"Is that so?" He glanced in the direction of the waitress, then back at her. "Sorry your search didn't turn up much."

"It turned up one interesting thing." She lowered her voice and leaned forward. "Jerry, wasn't actually Jerry."

"What do you mean by that?" He stared hard into her eyes. Then he held up one finger as the waitress returned with the food. Once she walked away, he looked back at her. "Well? What did you mean?"

"I think you know." She swirled her spoon in her soup. "Maybe we should both drop the act, and just be honest with each other."

"I wasn't aware that you were acting." He narrowed his eyes and smiled slightly. "You're good."

"I know that Jerry was living under a false identity, and I suspect that you knew this, too."

"Huh." He didn't touch his soup, or his sandwich, but only continued to stare at her. "You know an awful lot, don't you?"

"Too much?" She held his gaze.

"Perhaps." He sighed and pushed his plate and bowl away from him. "Look, this isn't the place to have this conversation."

"You have to eat, Detective." She pushed his plate and bowl back towards him.

"Arthur." He picked up his spoon and sank it into his soup.

"Arthur?" She blinked.

"My name is Arthur." He took a sip of his soup.

"Oh." She tipped her head towards him. "Nice to meet you, Arthur."

"Thank you." He picked up his sandwich.

"If we can't talk about Jerry's secret identity, then can we at least talk about your friendship? How is it that a man who was so disliked by everyone he knew, became your friend?"

"Jerry wasn't the greatest guy, that's for sure. But he did some good things in his life. Although, that didn't make him a good person, it still went a long way in my book."

"Like what? What good things did he do?"

"We'll discuss that after lunch. Now, I think it's my turn to ask some questions." He met her eyes.

"You haven't actually answered any of mine." She shook her head, then took another spoonful of her soup.

"You hid Brenda from me, didn't you? When I came to the house to talk to her?" He had a bite of his sandwich. "She was there, wasn't she?"

"Yes, she was." She put her spoon down. "And yes, I hid her from you. Because you were coming at her like a shark, and she doesn't deserve that kind of treatment. She was terrified."

"So you'd like to tell me exactly how I should do my job?" His tone sharpened.

"I'd like to tell you to stop wasting your time breathing down her neck when we both know there is something much larger at play here."

"What I know." He took the last bite of his sandwich, then leaned across the table towards her. "Is that donuts purchased from your truck, made by Brenda, were laced with poison. Every one of them from what we took from the bakery. It is only out of pure luck that only Jerry ate one and died from it."

Her heart lurched. Hearing the words from his lips made things even more vivid. If anyone else had eaten a donut, there could have been more bodies.

"Maybe we should step outside and talk about what we can't talk about here."

"You haven't finished your soup." He raised an eyebrow.

"I'm not hungry anymore."

"I don't blame you." He wiped his mouth with a napkin.

She reached for her purse to pay for the meal, but he had already placed a few bills on the table.

"I've got this."

"But I invited you." Joyce frowned.

"Sorry, I'm old fashioned, if a lady shares a meal with me, I pay the tab." He stood up and looked towards the front door. "Ready?"

~

*B*renda couldn't just stay at the house. Her mind was spinning a million miles a minute. Instead, she grabbed her keys and headed for the bakery. She wasn't going to just let the hand-cuffs clasp around her wrists. She had every reason to believe that Orville was the murderer. He had access to the bakery, he stood to gain the most from Jerry's death by inheriting the bakery, and he had motive due to the way Jerry treated him. Even if he was not the killer, she was certain he knew more about Jerry's life than he was letting on.

When she arrived at the bakery she found the door open, but the sign turned to closed.

"Hello?" She pushed the door open and stepped inside.

Orville stepped out from behind a stack of boxes.

"Great. What is it?"

"I just wanted to speak with you for a few minutes, if that's okay?" Brenda smiled.

"If it's not one, it's the other, huh? Why are you here asking me questions?" He looked at her with irritation as he rested his hands on the stack of boxes. "Still trying to clear your name?"

"I had nothing to do with Jerry's death, I think you know that." She frowned as she studied his expression. He seemed to be hiding something. "Out of everyone in this town, I'm certain that you knew Jerry best. Did you know that his name wasn't Jerry? That he had a secret identity?"

"I don't know what you're talking about." He shook his head and moved another box onto the stack.

"I think you do. He trusted you, why else would he have left the bakery to you?" Brenda stepped in front of the boxes to block his path to the stack. "This is important, Orville. Someone murdered Jerry, and I'm not the only one that is a suspect."

"I have an alibi. I was with someone the whole time, from the time I left the bakery till that morning. We even went to a movie. I have the ticket stub to prove it." He set the box he held down on the floor and faced her with narrowed eyes. "I didn't hurt Jerry. I don't know if you did or not. You expect me to tell you things, when you might have been the one who killed him?"

"If I was, then why would I be here now? Why would I be trying to find his killer? It wasn't me, and it wasn't Joyce, and I think you know that." She searched his face for any clue he might offer. "But do you know who it was?"

"No." He sighed. He ran his hand back through his hair. "I don't know what to think about all of this, all right? One day Jerry was telling me that he never wanted to see me again, and the next, I'd inherited the bakery. It doesn't make sense to you? Well, it doesn't make sense to me, either. You're coming to me for answers, but I don't have any. I can only think he left it to me because he had no one else to leave it to. All I know is that Jerry didn't like to talk about his past. When he first moved here, he bought the bakery, and hired me. He wouldn't hire anyone else. Just me. I couldn't keep up, I asked him over and over again to hire someone else, but he refused. It wasn't until a few years in that he finally hired other people. I thought he just made enough money to afford it, but maybe there were other reasons."

"So the only person he trusted was you?" She met his eyes.

"Are you kidding?" He laughed as he stepped around her and headed towards the front of the bakery. "Jerry didn't trust anyone."

"What about girlfriends? He must have had some." She followed after him.

"Not one. I never saw him so much as smile at a woman. Now, if he did things after hours, I don't know about that. You're not getting the point. We weren't friends. We worked together every day, but we didn't go out and shoot pool, or have drinks. I've never been inside of his house. He's never been inside of mine. I tried to get to know him better, but each time I did he put up roadblocks, so I took the cue and left it alone. He wasn't exactly the type of person that someone would want to get to know. He was harsh, and cold, and had a temper that would flare over the stupidest things."

Frustration built within her as she realized that the most likely person that might have insight into Jerry's mind, in the entire town, was clueless about him. However, his final words lingered in her mind. If he got so angry over simple things, maybe that was a clue on its own.

"What kind of things would he get angry about?"

"Sometimes he would get a phone call, and it would set him off. I always assumed it was about bills, but he never said. Other times he would just fly off the handle and shut down the whole bakery for the day, sometimes a few days. He would never say why, he would just tell us all to get out. One time he even did it with customers in the bakery, he pushed them right out the door. It was ridiculous. He never gave any explanations."

"That's very odd behavior." Brenda crossed her arms. "It never struck you as strange?"

"Of course, it did." He rolled his eyes. "But people can be strange. It's not my business if they are. He paid me, so I did my job."

"Even though he was so harsh to you? Why did you keep working with him for so long if he treated you like that?"

"You haven't worked minimum wage jobs much,

have you?" He gathered some items from behind the counter and tossed them into a box.

"No, not really. Why?"

"When you work a minimum wage job, no one has to treat you nicely. Your bosses know that they own you, because you're completely dependent on your paycheck. Trust me, Jerry was not the worst boss I've ever had." He slid around to the front of the counter and looked her straight in the eyes. "If someone killed Jerry, your safest bet is to stay out of it. Got me? Don't you have a kid?"

"Yes." She was a little startled that he would know that. "A daughter."

"So wise up, lady, and forget about all of this. People don't get knocked off for no reason. You're digging yourself into the middle of something that could get you in trouble. Just leave it alone."

"Why would you say that? Do you think Jerry was mixed up with some dangerous people?"

"He was poisoned, wasn't he?" He settled his gaze on her. "Do you think kind, good upstanding citizens poison people?"

"No." She frowned. "But had you ever noticed anyone around him that might be capable of something like that?"

"People don't usually advertise that they're

murderers." He sighed. "No, all right? I didn't see this coming. No one did. It doesn't matter how many questions you ask me, I'm not going to have answers for you."

"Well, thanks for your time, Orville. Are you packing everything up? Do you plan to close the bakery?" She started towards the door.

"Yes. Closing it. Selling it. And getting out of this town." He sighed as he heaved another box onto the pile. "There's nothing here for me."

"Good luck to you, Orville." As Brenda stepped out the door and onto the sidewalk frustration boiled up within her. No matter where she turned it seemed as if there was nothing to find out about Jerry. In fact, as far as she could recall, only one person had described him as a friend. She wondered how Joyce's meeting with Detective Crackle was going.

As she approached her car, she noticed Gray's truck a few spaces away. Her heart skipped a beat. Aaron said Gray's truck was one of the vehicles he noticed in the parking lot that morning. She glanced around to see if anyone was watching, then crept up to his truck. Inside, she saw a few documents that included the address of the farm. Curious, she boldly opened the passenger side door. It wasn't locked, but she knew she was still breaking in, which was scary. She snapped quick pictures of the documents, then hurried off to her car. As she reached it, she saw Gray walking towards the parking lot. Her heart flipped. He waved at her, and shouted. She struggled to get her key in the lock.

"Hey!" He broke into a run as she pulled her door open. "Stop!"

She tried to get inside and close the door, but before she could, his meaty hand grasped the door frame and held it open. She held her breath as he leaned over the door and glared at her.

"Didn't you hear me? I thought you wanted your tree delivered today?"

"Oh, yes." Relief flooded through her. "Can we arrange it for the end of the week, now?"

"Sure."

"Thanks. I'll come see you to arrange it. I have to go now." She tried to disguise the fear in her voice.

"Suit yourself." He shrugged, then turned and walked away.

CHAPTER 14

As soon as Joyce stepped outside with Detective Crackle right behind her, she felt her nerves rattle. Being alone with him was strange to her. It created a sensation that she couldn't really identify.

"Now, tell me what you know." She turned to face him.

"I don't have to tell you anything." He held her gaze.

"Then this was a waste of time." She started to walk towards the parking lot.

"Wait." He grabbed her arm and tugged her back. "I don't have to tell you anything, but I'm willing to. Maybe that will help you to see that I'm not the enemy here."

"Maybe." She quirked a brow. "That depends on what you have to say."

"I can only tell you this now because Jerry is dead and can obviously not be in danger anymore." He frowned. "This doesn't need to be spread around town. I can get in trouble if it is. Can I trust you to keep this quiet, please?"

"Yes." Her eyes widened as she realized that was true. She wanted to protect him.

"Jerry was an informant on a case. He used to be part of a crime ring in a town where I used to live and work as a police officer. I caught him, and he agreed to help me bring down the ring. I assured him he would get police protection, that he would go into the witness protection program. I really thought he would. But once he turned all of his friends in, the District Attorney refused to approve him for protection. So, I took it upon myself to find him a place to go. I placed him in another state at first, but then I was transferred here. I never thought much about it, until he was attacked. I knew I had to get him somewhere safe, and this was the safest place I could think of, so I moved him here. I set him up with a new identity, got him started with the bakery, and assured him I would keep an eye on him." His expression tensed as he shook his head. "Clearly, I didn't do a good enough job."

"Wait, so you're saying Jerry was an informant? That's the good thing he did?" She searched his eyes.

"Yes, he put a lot of dangerous criminals behind bars. I'm afraid, one of them has tracked him down."

"But aren't they in jail?" She frowned.

"Some are, but some have been released. Three that I know of." He sighed. "It was a big ring and Jerry didn't know how far-reaching it was. Some were never caught."

"If you knew this, then why were you coming after Brenda?" She frowned. "You must have known it wasn't her."

"I wasn't coming after her. I had to investigate all suspects. I thought Jerry was safe. I didn't think anyone could find him here. I thought since it was her donuts that were poisoned whoever did this might be associated with her. Maybe her husband, or a friend, someone who had discovered who Jerry was or had managed to find him. But the more I investigate Brenda the more I think she wasn't involved." He sighed. "I'm no closer to finding the killer than I was when I started. And yes, Jerry was not a great person, but after years of trying to keep him safe, in a way he'd become family to me."

"I can understand that." She rested her hand on his shoulder and waited until he looked up at her, to speak again. "Detective…, Arthur." She held his gaze. "This wasn't your fault. Not any more than it was Brenda's, or mine. Somehow someone found him, and you couldn't have possibly known that. Whatever I can do to help you with this case, I will."

"Thank you." He reached up and touched the back of her hand that still rested on his shoulder. "I wish I could believe it wasn't my fault. But I was the one who wasn't paying attention. Now, the only thing I can do for him, and for this town, is to make sure that whoever killed him can never hurt anyone again."

"And you will." She pulled her hand away. "I'm sure of it."

"I appreciate your confidence." He studied her a moment longer, then glanced away. "Please, apologize to Brenda for me. I didn't mean to frighten her."

"I will." She watched as he walked towards his

car. Now she understood the intensity of his behavior. He wasn't just trying to solve a crime, he was trying to find justice for someone he was trying to protect, someone he considered a friend, and protect the town that he cared about from men he was certain were quite dangerous. Perhaps her rush to judgment about him was shortsighted.

As she reached her car her cell phone buzzed with texts from Brenda. They were pictures of documents that indicated Gray's farm was to be sold within a few days. Then another text came through from Brenda.

Gray is getting ready to leave town. The timing seems odd since he hasn't been here that long. Remember how the day of the vendors meeting was the same day that Jerry bought cameras? We weren't the only new vendors introduced that day. Gray was as well. I think it's starting to add up. Don't you?

Joyce stared at the text as her heart raced. If Gray had showed up in town recently, if he was ready to leave town again so soon, that would indicate he was leaving quickly for a reason. Could that reason have been Jerry? If that were the case, then he might just be one of the criminals that was involved in the crime ring, maybe Jerry even helped put him behind bars. She turned to call out to Detective Crackle, but his car was already gone. She thought about calling him to tell him her suspicions, but decided that before she could bring the theory to his attention, they needed some solid proof. If Gray got a visit from a police detective he might just leave town even faster. She texted Brenda back.

I'll meet you at the house. I think it's time for a fieldtrip.

Brenda was in the driveway when Joyce arrived. As they exchanged information that they'd discovered, Brenda climbed into the driver's seat of her car, and Joyce settled in beside her.

"So, you think we should go to his house?" Brenda looked over at her. "Isn't that risky?"

"It is, if he's there. But I doubt we'll get any proof otherwise. A man that lives that far off the grid keeps his secrets at home." Joyce nodded. "The only way we're going to find anything, is if we get inside."

"All right." Brenda drove towards the farm. She tried not to think about how hard her heart was pounding. Gray had frightened her enough earlier that day. Now the thought that he might be a hardened criminal and murderer made her even more nervous.

"Stop here." Joyce pointed to a small side road before they reached the driveway that led to the farm. "We don't want the car to be spotted when we go in."

"Do you think going in is wise?" Brenda frowned as she glanced in the direction of the farm. "If he catches us there…"

"He won't. We'll make sure of it." She pulled out her cell phone and dialed Detective Crackle's phone number. To her surprise he answered on the first ring.

"Joyce, how can I help you?"

"I need you to look into someone for me. Gray Spruel. He owns a tree farm, and sells trees at the holiday market."

"Sure, I have some locals investigating all the vendors and I was planning to speak to Gray today."

"Now would be a good time." She glanced over at Brenda, whose eyes widened. "Maybe you should call him down to the station for a conversation."

"Why?" His voice grew stern. "Have you found something new?"

"I have good reason to believe he was involved

in all of this. I suspect that he knew exactly who Jerry was, his real identity."

"Why do you think that?"

"Wouldn't you rather ask him?" She did her best to sound convincing as she spoke. "He showed up here, recently, and he is disconnected from the community."

"So, he's not friendly? That doesn't make him a killer."

"Wouldn't you take any lead? This is my hunch. Don't you think it's worth looking into it just in case I'm right?"

"I think you might be barking up the wrong tree. I found a possible connection between Orville and Jerry from years ago. They lived in the same area. I just need confirmation it was at the same time."

"So nothing has been confirmed?"

"No."

"Well, I think you should look into Gray in the meantime."

"All right, I'll look into him more closely."

After he hung up the phone, Joyce looked over at Brenda.

"I'm not sure if he's going to do it, but I planted the seed. We might just have to wait at the car for a while." She rubbed her hands together and shivered. "At least we can turn the heat on."

"Good idea."

As Brenda turned on the heat Joyce explained to her what the detective had said about Orville.

"Maybe we are wrong about Gray then," Brenda said. They were both startled by the sound of an engine roaring not far behind them. Brenda pulled Joyce down behind the dashboard, just as Gray's truck whizzed past. Had he noticed their car there? It was impossible to tell as he drove by too fast to see his face.

"Wow, I can't believe that worked." Joyce raised an eyebrow. "I guess Arthur trusts my hunch after all. Let's go take a look before he comes back."

"What if he changes his mind and turns around?" Brenda hesitated as she lingered behind the car. "What if Arthur finds out that we broke in? That's just another reason I could end up in jail."

"This is the best way to keep us both out. All we need is proof that Gray is connected to Jerry, if we get it, then Arthur will be able to make the arrest. If you're too nervous you can stay out here with the car. Let me know if you see someone coming." She turned and started walking down the long, dirt road that led to the farmhouse.

"No way!" Brenda jogged to catch up with her. "I'm not letting you go in there alone."

"I didn't think you would." She winked at her. Despite the farmhouse being visible from the road, it took several minutes for them to traverse the driveway that led to it. "It's getting chillier." Joyce pulled up the collar of her jacket as an icy wind carried across her shoulders.

"It'll be dark soon and even colder, so we should be as quick as we can." Brenda stared at the front door of the farmhouse. "And have we considered how we're getting inside?"

"Don't worry, I can handle that." Joyce winked. She pulled a small pouch out of her purse.

"What's that?" Brenda peered at it closely as she unzipped it.

"I asked Davey's old partner to teach me how to pick locks." She pulled out a slender metal tool and began to work on the lock on the door.

"Why? In case you were kidnapped or held hostage?" Brenda's eyes widened.

"Eh, I'm afraid not." Joyce's cheeks flushed as she glanced at her. "It's because I keep locking my keys in the house. I thought about hiding a key outside, but the more I thought about it the more foolish I realized that was. So, I asked him to teach me how to break in."

"So you pick locks often?" Brenda's eyes widened.

"No, he just taught me last week. This is the first lock I've tried, besides my front door." She grinned as the knob finally turned.

"Amazing." Brenda shook her head as she stepped inside. She paused and listened for any evidence of a dog. The house was silent. It was small inside, with a combination living room and dining room, as well as a tiny kitchen. The only decorations were some paintings of landscapes on the walls. Everything was in place, but dusty. "Doesn't look like he has much company." She walked towards the kitchen while Joyce checked out the table beside the couch. Both women dug through every drawer and shelf they could find.

"There isn't much to see, is there?" Brenda frowned. "Even the refrigerator is practically empty."

"There's still the bedroom." Joyce led the way towards the bedroom. As she reached it, she grimaced and pulled up at her shoe. "Ugh, I think I stepped in something sticky."

"Sap." Brenda nodded. "From the trees." She

suddenly gasped. "Oh Joyce! It was him! I know it was!"

"What? How? Did you find something?" She spun on her heel.

"The sap! That's what was sticky near the eggs. He must have trampled on them when he peered inside to make sure that Jerry was dead!" Her heart slammed against her chest. "We shouldn't be here, Joyce, we have to go! If it's him, there's no way he went to the police!"

"Just calm down, Brenda I'm sure…"

Her voice was drowned out by the roar of an engine. It was Gray's truck, returning to the farmhouse, that no one knew they were at.

"He's here!" Brenda blinked back tears of panic. "We have to hide!"

"Okay, okay, let's just try to be calm!" Joyce tried to control the fear in her voice.

"In here!" Brenda grabbed her by the wrist and tugged her into the small closet beside the bed. It was packed with thick shirts and heavy jeans, leaving not much room for her and Joyce to fit in. Brenda sucked in her belly as much as she could and swore she would get back into exercising after the holidays. As she shoved herself back as far as she could against the wall, she heard heavy footsteps in the hallway. Her foot brushed against something on the floor. A bottle. She peered down at it just as Gray turned on the bedroom light. Enough light flooded through the crack in the closet door to reveal that the bottle contained white powder. Her stomach twisted as she realized that it might be the poison that had been used to kill Jerry. It further proved the fact that he was the killer. And they were about to be discovered by him.

CHAPTER 15

"He knows we're here," Joyce whispered as he drew closer to the closet. Before Brenda could respond, the knob on the door twisted.

"Get out here! Now!" He slammed the door open so hard that it struck the wall behind it with enough force to knock down one of the pictures he'd hung on the wall. As the glass shattered, Joyce's heart jumped up into her throat. She reached for Brenda's hand, just as the door swung open and light poured inside to reveal them both. The massive man stood before them with fury in his eyes.

"What are you doing here?" He grabbed Brenda by the arm and jerked her out of the closet.

"Stop! Let me go!" She struggled against him,

but she was no match for his strength. He easily tossed her down on the floor and reached for Joyce.

"Let you go?" He roared. "You're in my house! Did you break in?" He was not as rough as he grasped Joyce's arm, but he steered her out of the closet just as Brenda got to her feet.

"We were here to look for evidence to clear your name. To warn you. The police are coming after you!" Brenda gulped down a few breaths. "They're on their way here, now."

"The police?" He chuckled as he positioned himself between them and the bedroom door. "The police don't have a clue, and I'm no idiot. I know you aren't here for my sake. Now, what am I going to do with you?" He scowled at them both.

"Listen, you haven't done anything wrong. You're absolutely right. We're the ones who broke in, right?" Joyce tried to meet his eyes, but he began to pace, making it impossible. "Just call the cops on us. They're not going to believe anything we say. Trust me. That detective, he has a real problem with me. If you just call the cops, then all of our problems are solved."

"Except that if I call the cops, they'll know that you were digging around in here for something and the attention will be on me. They'll work out that I took revenge on my father's death." He shook his head, then paused directly in front of Joyce. "You shouldn't have come here. You should have let me have my privacy." He grabbed her hard by the arm, this time with far more pressure. "Now, I'm going to have to solve my own problems."

"Don't you touch her!" Brenda lunged forward and slammed her body into his. She knew that she wouldn't do much damage, but she had no idea what else to do.

"Real smart!" He growled as she bounced off his thick frame and stumbled until she collided with the floor. "Stay down!"

As he gazed down at her, his eyes blazing, and his lips twisted into a frustrated grimace, she realized what his intentions were. He wasn't going to risk letting them go.

"Gray, listen to me." Brenda stared up at him. "You can't do this. You're not a killer. Jerry had it coming, didn't he? You had a score to settle with him. But this isn't you. Jerry betrayed you. But Joyce and I haven't done anything to you."

"You broke into my house." He pushed Joyce down onto the end of the bed and kept one heavy hand on her shoulder. "You were going to turn me in to the cops. That's enough."

Joyce saw her opportunity. It wasn't a good one, but it was the only one she had. As he turned towards Brenda, she grabbed his wrist and elbow and twisted. In the same moment, she positioned her leg against his knee, and pulled him towards it. As she had hoped, he was shocked by the sudden pain, and thrown off balance. As he stumbled in an attempt to regain his balance, he met her leg. When she tugged with all of her strength, he toppled over her leg and landed hard on the floor.

"The bigger they are, the harder they fall," Joyce growled through gritted teeth, just as Gray started to scramble to his feet.

"Stay down!" Brenda shouted as she swung a lamp down against the top of his head. The man's body jolted, then collapsed against the floor. "Is he dead?" Brenda gasped as she stared down at him.

"No, just knocked out." Joyce grabbed her hand. "He's not going to stay that way for long, we have to get out of here."

"Maybe we should tie him up?" Brenda looked around for something that would hold him.

"No, there's no time. If he wakes up he'll over-power us."

"Should I hit him again?" Brenda winced.

"It's not necessary, Brenda, we just need to get

back to the car. I'll call for help!" Joyce pulled out her phone, only to find it had no signal. But it had at the car. "Hurry, we just have to get to the car."

"Joyce!" Brenda followed after her. "I found some white powder in the closet. I think it's the poison!"

"Good, that might be the evidence Arthur needs, but we have to get out of here alive."

As they bolted through the door, a shout came from the bedroom.

"He's already awake!" Brenda gasped. "He's going to catch us if we run towards the car, he'll see us."

"There's only one other option." Joyce looked towards the field of trees that spread out behind the farmhouse. An icy breeze made her shiver. It wasn't wise to go into the woods, as the sun was setting on a winter's night, but it also wasn't wise to be in view of a murderer. "Run, Brenda!"

They held hands as they ran towards the trees. Within moments they were past the tree line and deeper into the woods.

Brenda tried to get her bearings, to direct them towards town, but no matter where she turned, she saw the same towering trees.

"Joyce, I don't know where to go." She squeezed her friend's hand.

"It doesn't matter, just keep running." Joyce tugged her forward, deeper into the woods.

"But we won't be able to survive out here. It's freezing, and the sun is setting!"

"Our only other choice is to head towards that curl of smoke." Joyce paused long enough to jab her finger in the direction of the farmhouse they'd just fled. "If you think that's a wise idea, then maybe I was wrong about your instincts!"

"Shh!" Brenda squeezed her hand as panic seized her chest. "Someone's coming."

"Is it him?" Joyce whispered as she huddled close to Brenda. Then she could hear it, too. It was a subtle crunching of the leaves as he walked. She could barely take a breath as she realized that he may have already spotted them.

It seemed to take hours for a few seconds to pass. Gray's massive frame sauntered right beside them, but the light from the sun had faded, and they were well hidden by the trees. As he continued on, Joyce closed her eyes.

"He went past." She breathed a sigh of relief. "But who knows how long it will be before he comes back?"

"I don't know, but this is our chance. He's away from the house, and he probably won't return to it for quite some time. He is going to hunt for us. He's not going to expect us to head back that way."

"If we can make it back to the farmhouse we might be able to get a call out on the landline, if there is one. I have no signal here. Do you?"

"No, nothing." Brenda blinked back tears. "Should we try for the car?" She reached into her pocket in search of her keys, but found nothing. "Oh no, Joyce, I think I must have dropped the keys somewhere."

"It's okay, we're going to get through this." She hugged her friend. "Let's head back to the farm-house. The sooner we can call for help, the better."

As they approached the edge of the tree line, Joyce spotted a figure. It was too dark to make it out. She and Brenda froze.

"Who do you think it is?" Brenda whispered.

"Joyce? Brenda? Are you out there?" Arthur's voice drifted through the trees.

Joyce started to step forward, but Brenda pulled her back.

"Wait. How would he know we were here?"

Joyce considered the possibility for a moment, then shook her head.

"No. I trust him, Brenda. Hurry!" She pulled her towards Arthur. "Arthur! We're here!" She kept her voice low as she didn't want to alert Gray.

"There you are!" Gray's voice boomed from a few steps behind them.

"Run!" Brenda pushed Joyce forward towards Arthur.

Gray grabbed Brenda's shoulder and tugged her hard towards him just as she stepped outside of the tree line. She shrieked as she felt his strong hand threaten to break her bones. Then there was a loud bang. It made every muscle in her body jerk.

Gray groaned and crumpled to the ground.

"Brenda!" Joyce reached for her. "Are you okay?"

Dazed, Brenda looked back at the man on the ground. He'd been shot in the knee. As he rolled back and forth in pain, Arthur approached him with his gun still drawn. He kept the weapon trained on him as he barked orders into his radio for backup.

"I think the poison is in the house, Detective." Brenda stared into his eyes. "It wasn't me."

"I know, Brenda." He studied her with a frown. "I know."

As Joyce wrapped her arms around Brenda, she offered a small smile of gratitude to Arthur.

"It's okay. We're safe, now. We're safe."

As the dark, frigid night lit up with flashing lights of approaching police vehicles, Joyce held on to her friend.

Over the next hour they answered lots of questions, and Charlie arrived to see his wife.

"How could you do something so dangerous?" He cupped her cheeks as he looked into her eyes. "Brenda, why didn't you call me?"

"Charlie, it's okay, I'm okay. But please, I really want to see Sophie. I want to see my daughter."

"Okay, okay." He kissed the top of her head. "Let's go. We can start our holiday early."

Joyce shivered as she looked towards the farmhouse, which was crawling with police officers.

"All of us." Brenda took her hand. "Come with us, Joyce, we can spend Christmas together and give all of this time to blow over."

Joyce started to refuse. She never liked to intrude, but the look in Brenda's eyes filled her with warmth. Maybe her husband was gone and her kids were away, but that didn't mean she didn't have a family waiting to spend the holidays with her. As she walked towards Charlie's car with them, Arthur jogged up to her.

"More questions?" She looked over at him with an exhausted frown.

"No. I just want you to know that thanks to you, Gray, or should I say Paxton Jones, will never see the outside of a prison cell. His father died in prison and he blamed Jerry for his death because he ratted on him. I looked into him, but I wasn't able to link him to Jerry until today. We found the poison. When Jerry came to the vendors meeting, he saw him and recognized him. Gray couldn't believe his luck."

"Jerry must have recognized him or at least seen him loitering around the bakery. He was obviously worried, so he got the cameras."

"Yes, I think so. Gray recognized Jerry and he decided to take revenge and place you guys in the firing line. He overheard Mark mention that he got the donuts for Jerry to try and he snuck into the bakery and sprinkled the poison over the donuts." He looked at his hands. "I only wish I could have stopped all of this before it started."

"You did what you could, Arthur." She patted his cheek. "You saved us both. Brenda and I never would have made it out of there alive if you hadn't shown up. How did you know?"

"I was waiting on some information from some

locals and I figured out Gray's connection to Jerry. The lead on Orville was a dead-end and then Gray didn't show up for our meeting. Then I tried to reach you, and Brenda. Neither call would go through. My instincts told me that you had used me as a distraction, and I assumed that you were at the farmhouse." He stared into her eyes. "It was just a hunch. Then I saw your car."

"You have great instincts, Arthur Crackle." She smiled. "Merry Christmas, Detective."

"Merry Christmas, Joyce."

~

Two days later, Joyce sat on a couch in a friend's living room in front of a giant, over-decorated tree, and listened to the squeal of a little girl who believed in Santa. She watched as Charlie and Brenda fawned over Sophie. It was a moment that could have turned out to be far different. Her gaze wandered to the large living room window as she thought of Detective Crackle and what kind of holiday he might be having. Outside, the yard, and the street were blanketed in snow. The Christmas lights that adorned the houses in the neighborhood, sparkled against the pristine white world. The sight of it took her breath away.

"Isn't it beautiful?" Sophie slipped her hand into hers. She'd abandoned her pile of toys. "Want to build a snowman?"

For a split-second she thought about the cold, and the ache it might cause in her joints, but those thoughts passed in the glimmer of Sophie's eyes.

"Oh yes, let's do it!" She laughed as she followed her outside. The whole family joined in to make the snowman. Joyce took a step back and snapped a photograph of the moment. She sent it in a text to Detective Crackle, and wished him a Merry Christmas. He sent back a picture of his feet propped up by a fire, beside a cup of hot chocolate, and wished her the same. Despite the chilly temperatures, she felt a warmth grow within her.

Finally, the magic of the holidays had arrived, and as Brenda slipped her hand into Joyce's, she felt all of the stress of the past week fade away. She was ready to enjoy the holidays.

The End

❖ ❖ ❖

Thank you very much for reading 'Fatal Festive Donuts'. I hope you enjoyed it. You can sign up for my cozy mystery newsletter to be notified of my latest releases so you don't miss out on the special new release price at
http://www.cindybellbooks.com

BAKED GINGERBREAD DONUTS
WITH GINGER GLAZE

I have included recipes for both ginger glaze with sprinkles and a red, white and green glaze with ginger. You can use one or the other or make a mixture, depending on what you prefer.

INGREDIENTS:

Donuts:

1/4 cup butter
1 cup all-purpose flour
2 teaspoons baking powder
1 teaspoon baking soda
1/2 teaspoon ground ginger
1 teaspoon ground cinnamon

1/8 teaspoon ground nutmeg

1/8 teaspoon ground cloves

2 tablespoons brown sugar

1/2 cup buttermilk

1 egg

1 teaspoon vanilla extract

3 tablespoons golden syrup

Ginger Glaze with Sprinkles:

1 cup confectioners' sugar

1/8 cup milk plus extra to thin the glaze if necessary

1 teaspoon ground ginger

Red, white and green sprinkles for decorating

Red, White and Green Glaze:

1 cup confectioners' sugar

1/8 cup milk plus extra to thin the glaze if necessary

1/4 teaspoon ground ginger

Red gel food coloring

Green gel food coloring

PREPARATION:

Preheat the oven to 350 degrees Fahrenheit. Grease a 6-hole donut pan.

Melt the butter and set aside to cool.

Sieve the flour, baking powder, baking soda, ginger, cinnamon, nutmeg and cloves into a bowl. Add the brown sugar and mix together.

In another bowl mix together the melted butter, buttermilk, egg, vanilla extract and golden syrup.

Add the dry ingredients to the wet ingredients and mix until combined. Don't overmix, the mixture will be a bit lumpy.

Spoon the mixture into the prepared donut pan.

Bake for 12-14 minutes. The donuts are ready when a skewer inserted into the middle comes out clean.

To prepare the ginger glaze with sprinkles, whisk the sugar, milk and ground ginger in a bowl until well-combined. Add extra milk to thin the mixture if necessary.

When the donuts are cool, dip one side into the glaze and move around until the side is covered.

Sprinkle the glazed side with the red, white and green sprinkles and leave to set on a cooling rack.

To prepare the red, white and green glaze whisk the

sugar and milk in a bowl. Use extra milk to thin the mixture if necessary.

When the donuts are cool, dip one side into the glaze and move around until the side is covered. Take the remaining glaze and mix in the ground ginger. Divide the glaze into two. Using a couple of drops of food coloring dye one portion red and the other green.

Using a spoon, drizzle each color over the glazed donut. Leave aside to cool.

Enjoy!

ALSO BY CINDY BELL

DUNE HOUSE COZY MYSTERIES

BEKKI THE BEAUTICIAN COZY MYSTERIES

SAGE GARDENS COZY MYSTERIES

Snow Can Be Deadly

Tea Can Be Deadly

A MACARON PATISSERIE COZY MYSTERY
SERIES

Sifting for Suspects

Recipes and Revenge

Mansions, Macarons and Murder

NUTS ABOUT NUTS COZY MYSTERIES

A Tough Case to Crack

A Seed of Doubt

HEAVENLY HIGHLAND INN COZY MYSTERIES

Murdering the Roses

Dead in the Daisies

Killing the Carnations

Drowning the Daffodils

Suffocating the Sunflowers

Books, Bullets and Blooms

A Deadly Serious Gardening Contest

A Bridal Bouquet and a Body

Digging for Dirt

CHOCOLATE CENTERED COZY MYSTERIES

The Sweet Smell of Murder

A Deadly Delicious Delivery

A Bitter Sweet Murder

A Treacherous Tasty Trail

Luscious Pastry at a Lethal Party

Trouble and Treats

Fudge Films and Felonies

Custom-Made Murder

Skydiving, Soufflés and Sabotage

WENDY THE WEDDING PLANNER COZY MYSTERIES

Matrimony, Money and Murder

Chefs, Ceremonies and Crimes

Knives and Nuptials

Mice, Marriage and Murder

ABOUT THE AUTHOR

Cindy Bell is the author of the cozy mystery series Donut Truck, Dune House, Sage Gardens, Chocolate Centered, Macaron Patisserie, Nuts about Nuts, Bekki the Beautician, Heavenly Highland Inn and Wendy the Wedding Planner.

Cindy has always loved reading, but it is only recently that she has discovered her passion for writing romantic cozy mysteries. She loves walking along the beach thinking of the next adventure her characters can embark on.

You can sign up for her newsletter so you are notified of her latest releases at http://www.cindybellbooks.com.